HER HIGHLAND DECEPTION

HIS HIGHLAND HEART SERIES BOOK 7

WILLA BLAIR

OLIVERHEBERBOOKS

"One intriguing twist after another."

— AMAZON REVIEW

HIGHLAND ECHO

"...an amazing story that has every emotion you want to read in a story along with Highland secrets of special powers, finding the love they always desired while conquering their fears..."

— AMAZON REVIEW

HIS HIGHLAND HEART SERIES
HIS HIGHLAND ROSE

"Masterfully and brilliantly written Scottish Romance...!"

— MY BOOK ADDICTION & MORE

HIS HIGHLAND HEART

"The plot was honestly a masterpiece. It was well thought out and orchestrated. Right out the gate I was hooked! The hero had immediate book boyfriend appeal."

— LONG AND SHORT REVIEWS

"Willa Blair knows how to make a story come to life and sweep you away on a beautiful journey into the Highlands...This is a Scottish adventure you won't want to miss!"

— BOOKS & BENCHES

HIS HIGHLAND LOVE

"Beautifully written and masterfully executed!"

— MY BOOK ADDICTION AND MORE!

"Fiery passion burns bright in HIS HIGHLAND LOVE! Readers who enjoy Highland romance should definitely try Willa Blair's books."

— BOOKS & BENCHES

"If you love romantic highland stories of warriors and danger, love and honor, you'll find this story intriguing as well as enjoyable."

— THE READING CAFE

HIS HIGHLAND BRIDE

"Ms. Blair has delivered a wonderful and captivating read in this book where the chemistry between this couple was strong; the romance hot..."

— BOOK MAGIC, UNDER A SPELL WITH EVERY PAGE

"This is a very enjoyable and well-written book to satisfy any historical romance lover, especially one who enjoys forbidden love!"

— IND'TALEMAGAZINE

LAIRD OF LIES

"An immersive story with a smooth flow that drew me in and kept me engaged from start to finish. I read it in one day."

— NATIONAL EXCELLENCE IN STORYTELLING CONTEST JUDGE

LAIRD OF SIGHS

"Blair's narrative seamlessly embodies the essence of a love story, beautifully illustrating strength and compassion, culminating in a satisfying and heartening finale."

— AMAZON REVIEW

**HIGHLAND TALENTS SERIES
HEART OF STONE**

"...Fast paced and well written with passion, charismatic characters and romantic, thrilling storyline. Perfectly wicked and dangerous! Simply put, WOW!"

— MY BOOK ADDICTION AND MORE

"...you'll pick up to read again and again."

— READING BETWEEN THE WINES
BOOK CLUB

"With a little highland magic, anything is possible. I loved this story. A must read and now amongst my favorites."

— TIMELESS LOVE AND ROMANCE

HIGHLAND HEALER

"This is a great novel. Lovers of Hannah Howell's highland novels will love this."

— ROMANCING THE BOOK

"This story is action-packed and full of twists and turns that will keep readers on their toes. It is fast-paced and has a sweet romance that will warm your heart. Well written and full of imagination, this story is a must read for historical romance fans!"

— THE ROMANCE REVIEWS

"...a rich, enjoyable read."

— SATIN SHEETS ROMANCE

THE HEALER'S GIFT

"A Highland romance with a truly great hero...the story is compelling..."

— IND'TALE MAGAZINE

"A story of mystery, regret, hope, danger and trust...The characters are endearing, the story is fulfilling, and the set up for the remainder of the series presents an open invitation to dive right in. THE HEALER'S GIFT is a highly recommended read."

— FRESH FICTION

HIGHLAND SEER

"...this is different enough from other Highland romances to stand out from the pack. Ms. Blair's writing style is natural and evocative..."

— ROMANTIC HISTORICAL REVIEWS

"16th-century intrigue, muscled men with claymores and a doomed romance—is it any wonder I was reluctant to leave the rich, riveting world of HIGHLAND SEER?"

— USATODAY HEA

WHEN HIGHLAND LIGHTNING STRIKES

"Ms. Blair is a consummate storyteller...Can't wait for more from this magical author."

— MY BOOK ADDICTION AND MORE

"Ms. Blair has an easy to read talent for bringing a story to life."

— LONG AND SHORT REVIEWS

HIGHLAND TROTH

"Scottish romance at its best!"

— IND'TALE MAGAZINE

"...an exciting, romantic, historical tale full of angst, action and searing hot passion...With plenty of adventure and the twist of an old murder, HIGHLAND TROTH by Willa Blair, kept me hooked from beginning to end. A wonderful Highland romance."

— FRESH FICTION

CONTEMPORARY ROMANCE
WAITING FOR THE LAIRD

"Willa Blair spins a beautiful romance set in the Scottish Highlands full of suspense, history and mystery... I highly suggests you pick it up and enjoy."

— NIGHT OWL ROMANCE

"About 3:00 am I finally had to force myself to stop...yes, it was that good. Give yourself a treat and grab this book..."

— THE READING CAFE

"A contemporary romantic tale with a touch of history— and ghosts...Waiting for the Laird by Willa Blair is a delightful romance and unexpected adventure set in Scotland."

— BOOKS AND BENCHES

WHEN YOU FIND LOVE

"When You Find Love is a beautiful romance filled with combative personalities, a family curse and a love that can't be quenched. Character-driven plot with supernatural undertones make this a must-read. The ending was so fantastic, I didn't want it to end. If you love fantasy romance, you'll be smitten with When You Find Love."

— N.N. LIGHT'S BOOK HEAVEN

SWEETIE PIE

"Willa Blair is known for her Scottish historical paranormal romance. She changes genres with a modern Scottish lass who escapes to the Big Island of Hawaii. SWEETIE PIE is a delicious pupu - Hawaiian word for appetizer. Blair delivers a sweet novella that captures the Aloha spirit of the island."

— K. LOWE

"True love stories never have endings."

— RICHARD BACH

To Laird Peter, the one I love. Every day is a new beginning.

AUTHOR'S NOTE

The story of Calum Brodie and Ella Munro Ross begins in HIS HIGHLAND HEART (His Highland Heart Series). Calum falls in love with Ella at first glance. But after escaping a forced marriage, she has no interest in men and spurns his every advance.

In HIS HIGHLAND LOVE (His Highland Heart Series), Calum is blinded during the battle at Red Harlaw.

HER HIGHLAND DECEPTION begins there.

CHAPTER 1

JULY 24, 1411—A FIELD NEAR
HARLAW, FIFTEEN MILES WEST
OF ABERDEEN, SCOTLAND

Calum Brodie stood with his chief, Iain Brodie, and his best friend, Euan Brodie, on the ridge overlooking the empty field outside the village of Harlaw. They would soon fight for Domhnall of Islay, the Lord of the Isles, against the Regent of Scotland, the Earl of Mar, both of whom claimed the same Ross territory. "We're close enough to Aberdeen, like as no', townsfolk have come to watch the battle," he said.

"We've heard that Mar's men have been moving troops in this direction for days," Euan added.

Iain nodded toward Mar's troops massed on the other side of the field, a mix of knights in armor and men on foot dressed in rough clothing, carrying short swords, pikes, pitchforks, or whatever weapons they had to hand. Most looked little different from many in Domhnall's army. "Much of that lot are merchants and farmers, no' fighters. If we're lucky, they'll decide to blend in with the townsfolk and disappear."

1

"We can hope so."

"Aye, well, hope never won a battle, did it?"

Calum turned to face the men arrayed behind the Brodie laird. They were ready, weapons sharp and faces grim. But their eyes gave away their eagerness for the battle to begin. "Domhnall had best give the signal soon," he said to Iain.

Iain pulled his claymore from the sheath on his back.

The heavy longsword flashed, blinding Calum for a moment with the sun's reflection. Iain took great care with his weapon, much as he did with his clan, and always sharpened and polished it to shine. He wanted an enemy to see death coming for him.

"Let's show him we're ready, aye?" Iain looked over his clansmen and raised his voice, thrusting his claymore skyward. "Are ye here to watch or to fight?"

"Fight, fight, fight," rang out and echoed back from the nearby hills.

"For Brodie!" Iain called out when the noise died down and raised his blade again.

In answer, the Brodie oath, "Unite!", rang out and filled the field. The men broke into raucous cheers as other clans allied with them called out their war cries in turn. Calum, heart racing, yelled along with them, and grinned at Iain. He was a master at rousing his men.

Kenneth Brodie, Iain's tanist, his second-in-command, joined them as the cheers died down. "T'will be a good day," he said. "The fog has lifted. We can see every man they have and how they move."

A cold chill ran down Calum's back.

"Dinna say that," Iain scolded. "Lest ye curse us."

Kenneth frowned, then nodded. "Ye have the right of it. I take it back," he added and crossed himself.

Relieved, Calum studied the opposing force. Knights on horseback, mail glinting in the summer sunlight, were easiest to see, though Mar positioned them toward the rear of his massed spearmen. Domhnall's army vastly outnumbered Mar's, but Mar's knights could make up for their lack of numbers. Men on horseback moved faster. Reacted faster. Their steeds' hooves and teeth were often as deadly as the steel their riders carried. Domhnall's men would have to take them down as early in the battle as possible.

Calum would be glad when this fight was over. It should settle control of Ross territory that had been under dispute for years. Even though he'd met Ella Munro because of that dispute, he'd be glad to see it done.

Ella. Nay, he couldn't think of the lass today. He must concentrate on staying alive, returning to her so that he could, someday, win her heart. No matter how he tried, she gave him no encouragement, but he wouldn't stop. He understood what she'd been through when stolen by Ross warriors and forced into a marriage she didn't want. She needed to be in command of her own destiny. But he was determined that destiny would include him.

First, he must stay alive.

Finally, the order came. Calum roared the Brodie oath, his voice lost among all the others around him. Answering cries went up from the clans flanking them. From both sides of the field, a host of others immediately joined them. Bellows and thundering hooves filled the air as the two sides rushed at each other, Mar's cavalry galloping to the fore. Iain pushed forward, and Calum forced his way through allies to flank his laird. He fought alongside Euan and Kenneth, staying near Iain, charged with protecting him.

In moments, Calum lost himself in the rage of battle, the pull of muscle and sinew as he swung his blade, hot blood slick on his fist as he shoved aside a body he'd impaled and surged onward. Even as his sword crashed so hard with another that he felt it in his teeth, he was intensely aware of everything around him. Arms lifting, blades flashing in the summer sun, cries of battle and screams of agony, the clash and clang of weapons and shields, thunder of horses' hooves, neighs and equine screams of distress, the reek of sweat, blood and piss. It all blended into a single awareness, himself at the center, Iain, Euan and Kenneth near him. He did not notice time passing. He measured the progress they made by the number of foes surrounding them. The battle eddied and swirled as they fought off knights and farmers with the same ferocity.

A sudden lull in the numbers of men coming at them gave Calum a moment to catch his breath, chest heaving. He felt Iain move behind him, and the laird shouted a warning. They'd only looked away a second, but they'd let down their guard!

Iain and Kenneth fought Iain's attacker as Euan kept watch around them, and fought off another attacker who charged at Kenneth's back. As Calum turned to help defend his laird, his gaze sweeping around them, the stench of another danger filled Calum's nose. Suddenly, a man loomed on Calum's opposite side. Too close. He had only a moment to think that if they lost Iain because of it, he'd rather die here than live with the shame. He raised his sword to block the blow aimed at separating his head from his shoulders. Blades crashed and sparked, the clang loud enough to make his ears ring. Something hit his head and the left side of his face. Light flashed behind his left eye, then went dark.

He raised his blade, expecting a death blow at any second. He fought to see, searching. Where was his attacker? Where were Euan and Kenneth and Iain? Darkness closed in. Hearing the battle rage on around him, oblivious to his fate, he swung in a wide arc and met nothing but air. He overbalanced and fell to his knees. Before everything around him went black, regret filled his heart that he would never get the chance to wed Ella, to tell her how he felt about her. To admit he loved her. As he fell, with his last breath he whispered her name.

CALUM WOKE TO PAIN, feeling as if massive hands spanned his head, wrapping around it, fingers squeezing until his skull cracked. Unless thought leaked through his skull with blood and brains, it was too heavy to reach the surface. A strange whistling filled his ears. Below it, he heard a low groan. His? He couldn't move, couldn't even open his eyes. Horror made his belly roil. Something cool dripped onto his lips and into his mouth. He swallowed and went away, back into the blackness.

The next time he woke, the pain in his head spread to his eye, sharp and piercing. Had he been stabbed in the eye? He managed to lift one hand, intending to pull out the blade, but cool fingers forced his hand back to his side and a feminine voice said something he couldn't comprehend. Male voices rumbled in the background, blurred and indistinct below the whistling. Nothing made sense, so Calum let the world go away again.

This time, he came awake with the determination to find out what had happened to him.

"Ah, Calum, good morrow."

He knew that voice. He loved that voice. Ella! What was she doing on the battlefield? He struggled to open his eyes, to sit up, to find his sword and protect her, but a hand on his chest held him down.

"Dinna move, laddie," a firm, older, female voice commanded. Not Ella. Where had she gone?

"Ella…" He tried to open his eyes, but couldn't.

"I am here, Calum." Soft fingers wrapped around his and he relaxed. The women would not be on the battlefield unless the fighting was over and Domhnall's army won. When had they followed Iain's men from Brodie? Calum thought Iain left them safe within its walls, hand-picked men remaining to defend them.

"Iain?" He croaked out the name, dreading the news he might receive. "Kenneth? Euan?"

"Hale and nearby," the older voice replied.

He finally recognized the clan's healer's voice through the fog of pain in his head.

"What happened? Why canna I see? Who is making that whistling sound?"

"Ye were wounded, lad, as ye ken."

Mhairi's tone was matter-of-fact. Calm. Yet Ella's cool fingers tensed on his hand.

"How bad?"

"A crack to yer heid, and ye can be glad 'tis so hard, ye yet live. But the sword that did it shattered, possibly on yers, no' on yer skull. Ye caught a sliver of steel in yer eye. 'Tis gone now."

"Then why—"

"Yer eyes are covered and bandaged round yer heid. Ye must rest and heal if ye hope to see again out of that eye."

Her comment stopped him from trying to lift a hand to his face yet again. "How long?"

"Another sennight, I think. Or a wee more. I'll judge as ye go," she told him. "Ella, go fetch some broth from the kitchen. Our lad is awake enough to drink, and it will help him heal."

Ella squeezed his hand, and the swish of fabric told Calum she'd done as the healer asked.

"Ella will care for ye, and see to yer needs," the woman continued, "until ye can do for yerself. Ye must stay abed and keep yer head still."

Calum didn't like the sound of that. "Nay," he said, forcing the word between dry lips. "Nay Ella. I'll no' abide her seeing me like this. One of the lads can attend to me."

"If that is what ye wish." Mhairi's voice communicated disappointment. "And here I thought ye pined for her. Months ago, ye confided in me that ye wished for her to be yers. Now that ye need her to help ye, and to comfort ye, ye dinna want her?"

"I do wish it," Calum insisted once the healer's complaint ran down. "But nay like this. Send Ella away, back to Brodie. She doesna belong on the battlefield with all the dead. The blood…"

"Lad, we are at Brodie. Ye are in yer own bed. Where did ye think…"

Shock turned his blood to ice, then he warmed again. They were safe. "I thought…the battlefield. Outside Aberdeen. How did I get home?"

"In a cart," Mhairi answered quickly. "Fortune smiled on ye, and ye made the journey safe in Hypnos' arms, unaware of yer pain. Ye came to me only a pair of days after ye took yer wounds. Iain made certain ye were cared for until ye arrived. Ye've had a little fever, and if ye do as I say, ye'll have nay more. But ye must do as I say. To save yer sight, ye canna move yer head overmuch. Do ye ken?"

"How have…how will I…" Suddenly he didn't want to know what had gone before, while he lay here, insensible.

"I'll send someone to see to ye, and check on ye myself, often. Dinna fash, lad. All will be well."

Calum heard her words but they faded into a well of sound, as if she moved far away from him, under the whistling instead of in front of it. He wanted to reach for her, to pull her back, but she'd said not to stir. So instead, he faded away, too.

"Dinna go in," the healer who waited for Ella outside Calum's door told her. "He sleeps again, and we must speak." She gestured for them to move away, down the hall.

Was something wrong? Ella frowned at her, then set the heavy tray she carried on the hallway floor as Mhairi closed the door to Calum's chamber. "About what?"

The older woman took her arm and led her toward the stairs she'd just climbed. "Now that he's awake, he doesna want ye to care for him, to see him…" She paused and frowned at the door. "The way he is now."

"But…" She'd been caring for him since he was brought home, just as she'd been helping Mhairi for months with the clan's ill and injured. Calum knew that. The only difference between him and others in the clan she'd tended was that he meant more to her.

Did he know that?

She'd always been shy around men. More so since she'd been kidnapped last year. But since she'd escaped and come to Brodie with her friend Muireall, who married Calum's friend Euan, she'd learned to trust Calum. He was her one male friend, and she wanted to find out where the feelings they did have might lead.

Mhairi pursed her lips. "Ye are no' married, and he has intimate needs unfit for a lass no' his wife or a healer or servant."

"I'm well aware." Ella canted her head, wondering if the healer had forgotten who'd helped her take care of his needs before now. Or if Calum was too confused by the blow to his head to recall that she'd been stolen from Munro and married to a Ross against her will. Men had few secrets from her. "I dinna care about that. I care about him."

"I ken ye do, lass. Ye have no' left his side since he was carried in and put to bed. 'Tis glad I am to ken ye return his affection enough to wish to do this. But now he's awake and uncomfortable with ye tending him…" She shrugged. "Though ye have helped me, ye have no' yet agreed to become my apprentice. I must do as he asked and find a serving wench to keep watch over him."

"Nay!" The idea of another lass having such close contact with him made her uneasy. Another lass would not care about him—or for him—as she did. "Wait, ye said I return his affection. What do ye ken that I dinna?" Earlier, Muireall said much the same, but it wasn't that he'd asked for her hand, or even made any grand gestures that made it clear to all that they were a couple. Still, there was something between them she couldn't yet define.

"'Tis no' my place to say, lass. Better a conversation best held betwixt the two of ye, aye?"

Ella swallowed her objections. Mhairi was right. Calum's friendship, his kindness, and the many ways he indulged her wishes were things she'd come to depend on. She didn't want to lose the closeness she'd never enjoyed with any other man, not even with Dermott Munro, the clansman she thought she loved and expected to marry before the Ross raiders kidnapped her, Tira and Muireall. After she returned home, he publicly refused to honor their betrothal, saying she was ruined by being kidnapped and forced to marry Thomas Ross. She was better off without Dermott. But what if Mhairi was wrong about whether Calum harbored any tender feelings for her, and he developed them for his caretaker? "Must it be a lass?"

"A lad then," Mhairi offered. "What else would ye have me do, Ella? A lad can stay with him and fetch me—or ye—if the need is urgent. I canna spend all my time with Calum. Others need my skills. Yers, too. And even if ye agree to become my apprentice, I think Calum will still prefer another see to him."

"Aye, I ken it." Ella crossed her arms and leaned against the wall at her back, thinking. For months, she'd put off Mhairi's offer of apprenticeship and the stability such a commitment would mean for her future. She had found friends here, but she'd never been certain how she fit into Brodie, or how she wanted to. Or even *if* she wanted to. So much had happened to her in a short time. What would it take for her to feel confident of a decision to spend the rest of her life here, in Brodie? Would it be better than going back home to Munro, or living somewhere else, or even after what happened to her, in Ross?

She owed the healer an answer, but not now. Calum came first. She wanted to be the one to care for him, but how could she when he didn't want her there? Thinking of growing up in Munro gave her the kernel of an idea. "What if he doesna ken 'tis I?"

"What do ye mean, lass? He kens ye well."

"I can change my voice, my gait, my touch, as I did when I was a lass playing with the other bairns at 'warriors and maids'." She cleared her throat and deepened her voice's pitch. "Do ye think he'd ken this voice?" She raised it to a high, clear, child's tone. "Or this?" She raised her open hands in a shrug while she waited for the healer's judgment.

Mhairi smiled. "The lower pitch will serve ye better, especially if ye speak softly. Dinna be as gentle with him as ye have in the past." She regarded Ella's hands, then took one of them and stroked it from palm to fingertips, making Ella's fingers curl. "'Twould help if yer hands were rougher."

Excitement set her pulse to racing. Could this work? "'Tis easily done. Today, Annie has set the maids to making soap. If I help them, the lye will do what's needful, and quickly." The Brodie lady would welcome another pair of hands to help with the onerous chore.

"Go on with ye, then. Ah, wait a wee. What shall I call ye?"

That was easy. "Janet. Call me Janet. 'Tis a common enough name for a lass."

"Soap," the healer muttered. She closed her eyes and sniffed. "Does he ken yer scent?"

"I…perhaps. I kenned my husband's and hated it."

"Of course ye did. He was forced on ye. Ye had every reason to hate him." She rested her chin on her hand for a moment. "We must find something that will give ye—give *Janet*—a scent all her own. An herb or spice rubbed into yer clothes might serve. Something pleasant or something strong?"

"I dinna want Calum to be drawn to Janet's scent."

The healer grinned as Ella pushed off from the wall with her elbows. "I'll make certain of that."

HOURS LATER, Ella carefully wiped her sore hands on her apron before she left the soap making area the laundress set up in the bailey. She'd deliberately splashed lye on them to roughen them. In that, she'd probably done too much. Between the lye and the wooden paddles used to stir the boiling soap, a few blisters were forming that would likely pain her for days, along with rough and irritated patches that might make convincing calluses on *Janet's* hands. But the pain would be worth it if Calum allowed Janet to tend him.

Thank the saints they made soap outside. She couldn't imagine how irritating it would be inside the keep, both to the women making the soap and to others if the smells filled the halls. At least out here, thanks to the laundress' careful planning, the wind blew the stench out of the bailey and away from the keep.

As it was, her eyes stung, worse even than when Mhairi made the tinctures and poultices she used. The fumes wafted up from the huge pot she'd tended, forcing her to keep blinking to try to clear her vision. She could sympathize with Calum's pain. Tears streaked her face, much the same as the other women around her. She turned her face into the breeze, letting it cool her burning eyes.

The healer joined her as she stood waiting for some relief.

"Let me see yer hands, lass," she ordered.

Ella blinked aside a few more tears and held out her hands for the healer's inspection.

"That should do nicely," the woman told her. "Ye've done enough to them for today." She held out a small pot. "Put a little of this on them to soothe the pain. Not too much. Ye want them to heal rough, and this will soften them. How are yer eyes?"

"Ye can see they're tearing."

The healer studied her for a moment and nodded. "That will pass soon. Ye didna actually burn them. They just feel that way."

"I'm even more sorry for what Calum has been through after this," Ella told her as she carefully dipped a finger into the pot the healer held and spread some of the concoction on her blisters, sighed as the pain eased, and then took care of the other hand. "That's better."

"The laundress and her lasses use it. It serves them well."

"I believe ye."

The healer offered the small pot to her. "Keep it. Likely ye'll want to use some before ye go to yer rest, or the pain in yer hands might disturb yer sleep. I have more for the other lasses."

"Thank ye," Ella told her as she carefully cradled the pot in her injured hands.

The healer nodded and moved toward the other women to check on them.

Ella turned for the keep. It was almost time for the evening meal. Would she be able to taste her food? She hoped so. She looked forward to getting the smell and taste of the boiling soap out of her nose and mouth.

Her friend Muireall intercepted her in the great hall

and wrinkled her nose. "Ye smell like lye and animal fat. What have ye been doing? Helping the laundress make soap?"

"Aye, exactly that." Ella shrugged and spread her arms. "I'm going to my chamber to change. I hope that will help get rid of some of the stench."

"Why would ye do such a thing? Have ye no' enough to do taking care of poor Calum? Ach, and look at yer poor hands!"

Ella displayed the healer's wee pot. "I have something to soothe them. Come with me and I'll tell all. I need yer help."

Muireall held her peace while they walked upstairs to Ella's chamber.

Ella set aside the pot of medicine, stripped out of her apron and dress, then wet a rag and wiped down her face, arms and, gently, her hands.

That done, she pulled another dress from the chest where she kept her clothes and made ready to go back downstairs. But instead of leaving the chamber, she sat beside Muireall on the bed.

"Are ye ready to talk?"

Muireall had to be curious, and Ella could count on her to be circumspect with what she was about to share with her friend. "Aye, very well, I am. And aye, I had plenty to do taking care of Calum."

"Had?"

"That's why I need yer help." In a few words, she explained Calum's reaction to having her care for him, and the scheme she and the healer devised to keep him from recognizing her until the bandages came off his eyes.

Muireall leaned back and regarded her under a crinkled brow. "Ye've gone barmy. Do ye really think that will work?"

Ella nodded. "Mhairi seems to think so. She's going to find a way to disguise my scent. With my voice and touch altered, my hands roughened," she said and held them up to display the damage she'd done to them, "it might work."

Muireall grimaced. "Ye need to put more of what's in that pot on them if ye want to be able to use them at all. They look bad. And why no' let the lads see to him? With their help, the healer can make sure he's getting well. Ye can visit. Ye dinna need to be by his side all the time. And Calum may no' appreciate yer scheme when he finds out. And he will."

Ella shook her head, but she did as Muireall suggested, smoothing the concoction on her palms and sighing as the pain eased. "I ken that, but...he helped save ye—and truly, me, as well. And he has befriended me. I canna do less for him. I need to be there. I owe him."

"And ye care for him."

"Aye. And ye have pointed out a few times that ye think he cares for me." A hint of warmth spread from her chest to her throat and face as she recalled Mhairi asserting the same thing. Did he? Could there ever be more between them than simple friendship? "I think 'tis why he's suddenly shy of being seen as less than strong. Less than who he is when he is well."

Muireall clasped her hands in her lap as Ella set aside

the pot of medicine. "He doesna want to disappoint ye. 'Tis understandable. But how do ye think he will feel when he learns ye disregarded his wishes? And lied to him?"

Ella's chest tightened. Muireall was right. She was going to go against Calum's wishes and he might be angry. Embarrassed at the least. Why not let the lads tend to him? The idea made her belly ache. "I canna leave his care to others. I'll deal with his reaction when the time comes. Right now, he needs help from someone who is devoted to him. No' a one of the serving lads or lasses truly ken him, or what he must overcome to retain his place in the clan."

Muireall sighed. "'Tis against my better judgment, but ye are determined. I see that. So, how can I help?"

"I need ye and Euan, as well as Annie and Iain and anyone else who has contact with Calum while he's healing to call me *Janet* if I'm in the chamber with him."

"Call ye Janet? That is all?"

"And act as if ye ken Janet. As if she has been a serving lass in the clan for a while."

"And if he asks why he doesna ken her before now?"

Ella held up her hands and laughed. "Tell him she works with the laundress. Surely he's never spent time there. Nay a man in his right mind would."

CHAPTER 2

Calum heard Iain and Annie's voices before they reached his chamber. He'd been awake and aware only a day, but in that time, these would be his first visitors. He didn't know what took his friends so long to put in an appearance, especially Euan, but he strongly suspected the healer had warned them away until he felt better.

He did feel better, but well enough for the Laird and Lady of the clan? He rubbed a hand over his bristly chin. He must look like hell. Why would Iain bring Annie to see him like this? His temper started to simmer again. It had been just under the surface ever since he woke up the first time. Ever since he'd learned of his injuries and Ella's part in caring for him. The idea still incensed and embarrassed him. And made the pain in his head even worse. And now Annie would see him at his worst as well. He wanted to shout at her to stay away. For Iain to return her to their chamber, but it was too late.

"Calum."

Iain's voice broke through the rumble of his thoughts. He tensed, waiting for Annie to greet him, too, but she didn't. Did he really look so bad that she was speechless? Or was her voice lost in the persistent ringing in his ears and the packing in them that the healer insisted would help the noise diminish by softening the sounds around him. All it seemed to do was make him half deaf as well as blind.

"Annie wanted to wish ye well, but I sent her away," Iain said before Calum could object. "I didna think ye'd want her here. No' yet."

Calum took a breath and let the tension ease out of him. He should have known Iain would understand his reluctance, even though Annie was probably determined to personally ensure he was being well taken care of. Or perhaps, Annie recognized that he would be uncomfortable with her presence, so Iain hadn't had to say much to dissuade her from coming. "Thank ye. I dinna. I'm no' fit company for any lass."

He heard Iain shift, then pull a chair from the hearthside nearer to Calum's bed. "I heard ye ordered Ella away from ye. She was only trying to help ye. She's worried for ye."

So this was why the laird had come—to chastise him for mistreating Ella?

The thought made his temper rise again. "She can worry as well from a distance as underfoot."

"Is that really how ye want it, Calum? I ken ye care for her."

Calum shifted. Why would a woman want a man who was weakened as he was, possibly forever?

"Nay, dinna try to sit up." Iain put a hand on his shoulder, not pushing him down but enough to hold him in place. "The healer told me ye are to stay as ye are, or ye risk yer eye."

Calum pushed out a frustrated breath. "I'll be lucky if by the end of this I can move at all, much less see out of two good eyes."

"We all pray ye will, lad. 'Twill no' be much longer before ye are up and about, back to training and keeping Brodie safe."

"I appreciate the encouragement, laird, but I dinna yet believe it."

"Believe this, then. Annie and I, Euan and Muireall, Kenneth and his new bride, Catherine Rose, and aye, Ella, even after ye denied her, are all here to help ye. As ye would do for any of us. Ye have only to tell us what we can do for ye. Rest and get well. As yer friend, 'tis all I ask. As yer laird, 'tis all I command ye to do."

Calum's eyes filled, and for once, he was glad they were covered by layers of cloth so that Iain couldn't see the way those words affected him. Calum's voice nearly betrayed him as he thanked Iain, the words coming low and gruff.

"Iain. Calum," Euan's voice interrupted them with brief greetings, breaking the tension.

Iain stood. "I'll leave the two of ye to talk. Be well, Calum," he added and left the room.

Euan waited while Iain's footsteps faded away before he took the chair the laird vacated. "Ye are a mess, my lad."

"Tell me aught I dinna ken. Last year a broken arm. Now this. What's next?"

"Naught, I hope. Ye are already ragged enough to frighten bairns and lasses, I'd say."

"I need a bath and aught done about this," he added, rubbing his scruffy lower face that the bandage over his eyes didn't cover.

"Aye ye do, but I'm more a mind of the anger seeping out of yer pores and making yer fists clench even now."

Calum forced his hands to relax. He hadn't been aware they'd tensed. As had his jaw. He loosened it and took a breath through his mouth. "I think I have a right."

"Aye, ye do. But to take it out on the woman ye've been trying to attract for the last year?"

"Ye willna say anything to her."

"Nay, of course no'. 'Tis yer place to tell her how ye feel, whether 'tis welcome or no'. Is that what is taking ye so long? Or is this because of Marjorie again?"

Calum didn't want to think about her, or to answer that question. He'd been unlucky in love in the past. Worst of all with Marjorie Lindsay, the seemingly sweet, biddable and caring lass who'd lied about her purity. She was already carrying a married man's child and to escape the scandal, urgently needed to wed. Fortunately, the rumors had gotten back to Brodie before Calum offered for her. Dismayed, he confronted Marjorie. "Ye recall how she lied to me and claimed the rumors about her were false." She'd claimed they were spread by another lass jealous of her impending marriage to him. But Marjorie's maid, hearing about the tale her mistress told him, came to him to make sure he knew the rumors were true. After, he'd confronted Marjorie again and she'd confessed her plans.

"I do, and I also recall the other lasses ye pushed away because ye didna trust any who seemed too eager to make ye hers. An heiress for one. She was a baron's daughter, aye? And several lovely lasses, though their beauty didna rival Ella's."

Ella's reluctance over the last year to grow closer to him kept him from pushing her away, too, despite how she otherwise appealed to him. He knew her story. He'd been present when her husband returned her to Munro and repudiated her. Their sudden divorce shocked everyone, but he was glad for her and had spent the last year getting to know more about her. Yet, he still didn't know if she truly returned his interest beyond friendship or not.

He told himself she needed time to get past the trauma of that experience, and until she did, he would remain a friend, keeping her at arm's length for her sake. His injury had added another layer of distance, one he needed, because he didn't want her to pity him. "So everyone kens I refuse to let her care for me?"

"Everyone who counts, aye. Annie's quite cross with ye, and ye ken that's no' a place any man wants to be."

Calum snorted. "Iain didna mention that." He shrugged. "What can she do to make this worse? I already dinna ken if I have a future."

This time Euan snorted. "Feeling sorry for ourselves, are we? At worst, ye have one good eye. At best, two of 'em. Why no' wait until ye find out which it will be before chewing the leg off anyone who wants to help ye?"

"No' anyone. Just Ella." Had her kind nature fooled him? Did she think of him only as a friend to her, the same as anyone else in the clan she'd be determined to care for, rather than thinking of him as a man she might want for her husband? Had he misread her all along?

"So ye'd let Muireall or Annie—"

"Nay."

"Ye make my point for me."

"Do I?"

"There's aught Iain didna tell ye, or ye'd have mentioned it by now."

Calum stilled. "What?"

"We just came from a meeting in the solar. Iain, Kenneth, me, the other scouts—"

"I dinna like the sound of this." Despite the assurances Iain had just given him, Calum's gut twisted. Had they discussed removing him from the ranks of the scouts?"

"'Twas another incident like the one Kenneth and Cameron Sutherland just got into."

"What happened to Kenneth?"

"They encountered Irish gallowglass warriors, and to help Kenneth protect Cat, Cameron tried to lead them away, fought, and was wounded. Kenneth is fine. Now, we've heard one of the Gordon warriors has been injured in a fight with some men who were passing through Gordon land a few days after Harlaw. The lairds are no' happy about the remains of the two armies causing trouble."

"And no' kenning where that trouble is heading, I'll wager," Calum said, on the one hand relieved that his fear hadn't materialized, but on the other hand, angry that his condition meant he'd been left out of an important strategy session. How many more would he miss before he recovered? If he recovered. "I shouldha been there."

"With the Gordon?"

"At the meeting, ye *bampot*."

"Ye're no' ready for that, and Mhairi would have Iain's head if he got ye involved too soon."

"I've naught else to do but lie here and fash myself blind."

"No' funny, Calum."

"Ye try lying here for a sennight or more in the dark and see how ye feel about it."

"I wouldna like it any more than ye do. But I'd accept help where it was offered."

"So, back to the lasses, aye? I guess that proves ye are a better man than I."

Euan stood.

There was no mistaking the sound of it. Calum stifled a groan. Now he'd angered his best friend, too.

"I'll see to ye tomorrow. Perhaps ye'll be in a better mood by then. In the meantime, think on this: ye are a valued member of this clan. Ye have an important future here. A good life ahead of ye. It might no' be the one ye thought ye'd have, but ye will adapt. And yer friends will help ye—if ye will let them. And ye should. 'Tis what friends are for. Now get some rest."

He walked out before Calum could think of a reply that didn't involve every curse word he knew, or completely unmanning himself by bursting into tears.

"Iain should be here soon," Annie reported as Ella joined her and her sister Catherine at supper in the great hall.

"So should Muireall, Euan, and Georgie," Ella told them as she slid onto the bench across the trestle table from them. "Kenneth, too?"

Cat shook her head. "He's on the wall walk checking on the guards," she said.

"We dinna want any surprises," Annie added, her expression grim as she took a sip from the cup of ale in front of her. "There are still too many strangers passing through the area after the battle at Harlaw."

A chill ran down Ella's spine. "They should be Domhnall's men, aye? We fought with them. They should be welcome."

"They should," Annie said. Her expression as she glanced at her sister made it clear to Ella that it might not always be the case. Annie knew something.

The realization reminded Ella that Cat and Kenneth hand-fasted before they left Rose to come here to Brodie. Kenneth and Cameron Sutherland escorted Cat home to Rose from St. Andrews. Their route took them near Harlaw within a day of the battle. In trying to protect Cat, Cam was badly injured by some fighters. He was still at Rose under Mary Rose's care. She also remembered hearing that some men the Rose invited inside their walls threatened Cat. Kenneth saved her from being stolen, and probably worse, if the bastard who tried to abduct her had escaped the keep with her.

Annie clearly expected more trouble. Ella pursed her lips, acknowledging what Annie had not said, then pulled her gaze from Annie's and nodded her thanks to a serving lass who set a cup of ale in front of her.

"Supper's coming," the lass told them without looking at any of them as she stepped away.

Cat grinned and shrugged. "Soon, I hope. I'm famished."

"Are ye already carrying Kenneth's bairn?" Annie asked, her tone dry, but with a grin lifting the corners of her lips. "Famished is how ye'd be until ye delivered."

"Ye would ken," Cat teased. "But nay, no' yet."

Annie was expecting her and Iain's second bairn. Ella envied them their happiness. Her own future was much less settled, despite Brodie welcoming her. Calum seemed in no hurry to move whatever was between them beyond friendship, and she wasn't comfortable around any of the other Brodie men, not in a way that might lead to marriage. They eyed her in a manner she knew well— wanting her. A few tried acting as her friend, much like Calum, but without his sincerity. Some even admitted to wanting a lass who looked like her and who would make them seem better or more desirable to others in the clan.

She'd been subjected to enough of that in her life. Calum's friendship might evolve more slowly than she expected, but unlike the others, he didn't put any kind of pressure on her. And for that, she was grateful. But she still waited, which was one reason she had not committed to becoming Mhairi's apprentice. She longed for the kind of love her friends shared with their husbands, but she might never find it with Calum. Someday, Iain might have to betroth her to a man in another clan.

And that thought gave her chills.

True to the serving lass's word, she delivered bowls of stew before the sisters' teasing escalated. They both dug in.

Ella took a moment to enjoy the scent. Venison stew, rich with vegetables from the summer garden. She hoped Calum was getting some of this and Mhairi would let him sit upright enough to eat it. It would do him a world of good. She took a bite and savored the meaty flavor, distracted for a moment when another lass brought hot bread and a pot of butter to slather on it.

She set her spoon aside and reached for some bread in time to see Iain, Euan, Muireall, and Muireall's young half-brother Georgie approaching. She gave Georgie a grin. He'd grown so much in the year he'd spent fostering at Brodie, both in height and in confidence. Annie began training him as soon as he arrived, and it showed. Lately, she'd turned him over to Euan to join the rest of the lads his age, telling Georgie she'd done all she could for him and he was ready for whatever Euan would throw at him. So far, he looked to be handling his new status well. He grinned back at her before sitting on Annie's side of the table.

Ella turned her attention to the adults with him. She should know by now not to let Iain's expression worry her. He often looked stern. At the moment, he looked troubled. She looked to Muireall, hoping for reassurance that Calum was better, but her friend looked no less disturbed. Ella's appetite fled, but she held her peace while they settled, Iain giving Annie a kiss on her cheek as he sat beside her.

Annie must have noticed how their approach disquieted Ella. She turned to Iain and Euan. "What did ye learn?"

"He's in a dark place," Euan said as he and Muireall took seats beside Ella, "and I dinna mean the bandages on his eyes. He's angry and frustrated and worried."

Ella's heart broke for Calum, despite his continuing insistence that she—and all the lasses, save occasionally, Janet—stay away from him.

"He'll get better once the bandages are off and the healer tells him his vision will continue to improve," Annie, ever optimistic, said. Her gaze slid to the side to Georgie, telling Ella that Annie's comment was also meant to reassure him. Calum sometimes helped Euan with training, so Georgie would know him and be concerned about him, too.

"And if it doesna?" Ella couldn't help asking the question. "If she canna tell him that?" Ella feared Calum would not be able to adjust to a life where he was a half-blind man.

"We'll help him," Iain said. "We'll keep him so busy learning a new skill that he willna have time to feel sorry for what he's lost."

"Impossible. He's already there," Euan pointed out. "Imagining the worst."

"Wouldna ye be?" Muireall laid a hand on his arm. "Right now, Calum canna see. So, he canna see aught that is good."

They continued to talk while they ate, but Ella couldn't

stomach any food. Even Euan's confirmation that he checked on Calum again before coming downstairs, and that a lad now shared Calum's room to tend him didn't help. The longer this conversation went on, the worse she felt. She'd been told she possessed the beauty of one of the fae. She wished she had their magic as well. She'd wave a hand and heal Calum's eye, strip the bandages from around his head, and show him that all was well. But such wishes were futile. His future was up to the healer, and to how well he followed her instructions. "Feeling sorry for himself cannot help him heal," she said after having heard enough. "What can we do to ease his fears?"

Iain shrugged. "'Twill depend on what Mhairi lets him do. And how quickly. The sooner he can be up and moving, the better he'll feel. I ken that much."

Ella sympathized with Calum's frustration. She couldn't take sitting here listening any longer, stood, and stepped over the bench and away from the table. "I…that is, Janet, is going to see that the lad ye said is already with him has Calum properly readied for the night. I'll tell ye later how he is."

"Do ye need my help?" Euan made to rise.

Ella waved him back to his seat. "Nay. Finish yer meal. I'll see that the lad is taking good care of Calum and bid them a restful night."

"I'll tell Mhairi ye are going up," Muireall offered and stood. "Ye may need her to distract Calum, or to check on what her lad is doing herself."

Ella nodded, realizing Muireall was right. "Thank ye. All of ye. 'Tis hard to see someone we care for going through this, but with our help, he will get better." Surely her words disguised some of her feelings for Calum, even if they didn't hide her pain over what he was going through. The more she worried for him, the more she realized he wasn't just someone she cared about. He was more than that. But she feared putting a name to her feelings and making them real. She'd been through too much herself to be so bold. Not yet.

She pretended not to see the glance Iain and Annie shared between them. Instead, she walked away, head high, preparing herself for whatever confronting Calum might bring. Muireall's suggestion had been a good one. If Calum recognized her instead of accepting that Janet had entered his chamber, the healer's intervention might be needed.

She went first to her chamber and stuffed her pockets from the basket of onions she'd gotten earlier in the day from the cook, bit into one and chewed while she thought. She looked forward to a time when this ruse was no longer necessary and she and her clothes no longer reeked of onion. Her friends tolerated it for her and Calum's sake, but no doubt they'd be glad to see the end of it, too.

Especially if that meant Calum was healed and himself again. Let that day come soon.

She twisted her hands together and winced at the pain. The blisters had gone down, but the soreness remained in the roughened skin and tired muscles. The lye and constant stirring with the wooden paddles had done their job. Janet would appear—and feel—as though she worked with her hands on a regular basis. The pain distracted her, but she needed to wait until she returned to her chamber to use more of the healer's potion to ease it.

Decided, she went down the hall to Calum's chamber and knocked on the door.

"Come." That voice wasn't Calum's. One of the healer's lads, as expected, was sitting with him.

She remembered just in time to pitch her voice to Janet's deeper and softer tones rather than her own. "I'm Janet. The healer has asked me to check on ye. I've come to see if there's aught ye need." She lifted a finger to her lips to signal the lad not to question her name. Surely the healer would have instructed her lads about the ruse, but this one seemed young enough to be disconcerted by her presence. He might forget to use the proper name, which was why she'd identified herself as Janet first.

The lad opened his mouth, closed it and glanced at Calum, who appeared to be asleep, though with the bandages hiding the upper half of his face, it was hard to be certain. A plaid covered him from feet to chest, and he wore a leine that appeared as if he slept in it since he'd been brought home from Harlaw. She would make sure he was given a clean one in the morning.

"Ye can tell the lad to help me sit up," Calum suddenly said, his tone as surly as she'd ever heard from him.

"I canna do that. Ye must have the healer's permission."

"Then fetch her. I'm tired of lying here. I need to move."

"Can ye twist to either side without moving yer head? That might make ye feel better."

Calum started to roll onto his side.

"Wait!" Ella moved to the head of the bed and placed

her hands on both sides of his face, her sore, tattered palms firmly against his skull and her fingers tunneled into his hair above the bandage. That also put her pocket full of onions close to Calum's face. "I will hold ye," she told him. "Dinna try to turn all at once. Bend yer legs and let them drop to one side. Aye, like that. 'Twill relieve yer back."

Calum held the plaid in place under his arms and did as she directed. His answering groan told her it was working.

"Now, twist the other way. Ye, lad, come here and help him move."

With the lad shifting Calum's knees from side to side while Ella kept his head steady, they managed to give him some relief.

The healer walked in during their ministrations and stood, silently watching. The lad's back was to the door, so he didn't know she was there. She gave Ella a nod of approval.

Ella smiled, then turned her attention back to her cranky charge. The lad helped him move his legs as if marching while he lifted and lowered his arms. That was harder on her because even slow movement of his shoulders tended to make his neck and head shift, too, but she kept them steady.

When Calum tired, the healer made some noise to let the lads know she'd arrived.

Ella straightened as if surprised by her entrance.

The healer nodded and spoke up. "That looked helpful. Calum, how do ye feel?"

"Like I need to get out of this bed. How much longer must I stay here?"

"A few days more, then we'll see about ye carefully sitting up for longer and moving around this chamber. But for now, what ye were doing should help."

"Aye, it did, but I need to get up and move about. I dinna think I can stand days more in this bed."

"I ken it, lad. I'll have ye up as soon as 'tis safe. Now, thank ye, Janet," the healer told her, but her tone made it clear it was a dismissal.

Ella pursed her lips, tempted to argue, but no servant would gainsay the healer. She nodded and left the room to let Calum be readied for the night.

CALUM HAD SPENT many restless nights since his injury. Nightmares came often, replaying scenes from the battle that had blinded him. In some, he failed to protect Iain and watched his friend die, bleeding into the ground around his body. In others, he, too, died, after losing an arm or a leg, or suffering a sword strike to his gut and watching his innards spill out. Those were the worst so far and never failed to wake him, shaking and sweating and cursing the darkness he lived in.

But now, a new terror seized him. He prayed he was dreaming, and that he would wake from this scene. He feared he was losing his mind.

Ella stood before him, her luminous beauty undimmed, strangely visible despite the unrelenting darkness surrounding her. She glided toward him like one of the fae she resembled, hair and dress floating around her as though stirred by an unseen breeze. His heart hurt to see her. He wanted her more than he could say. More than he would admit to anyone, even to himself. More than getting his eye back. As long as he could see her like this, he wouldn't need it.

He knew that was wrong somehow. But watching her arm lift and her hand turn so her palm faced up, beckoning to him, he couldn't remember what it might be. He held out a hand, reaching for her, but blood dripped from his fingers. He'd ruin her dress. He pulled back his hand, ashamed to sully her beauty in any way.

She frowned and turned to the side.

When she turned back, everything about her had faded, the color leached from her clothes, her hair, her smile. Her beautiful face looked tired, dry, and her hands rough, as though she'd spent a lifetime toiling. Was this Janet? Where was Ella?

Suddenly she changed again, and he saw Marjorie, the lass who'd nearly ensnared him in a marriage to save her reputation. Only now her dress stretched over her belly, grown enormous and ripe with the child she'd tried to hide from him. What was she doing with Ella? Or with Janet? He didn't know what to make of this, but he didn't like it.

Suddenly, she was Ella again, but she turned from him. Because he was blind? No, that wasn't Ella, that was someone who looked like her who reached for him. Janet again? Were there really two women? This one looked like Ella, her beauty undimmed, but the hand that reached out to him was rough, her clothes homespun. Janet?

He said her name. Janet. She moved to him, raised her

face to his and kissed him. Her lips were smooth and warm, enticing him. How could he want Janet? He loved Ella.

When he didn't respond, she turned away, then turned back and was Ella again, face, hands, and clothing luminously beautiful, but disdainful, looking at him from the side of her eye as if not wanting to acknowledge him.

Janet wanted him, and Ella did not? What kind of nightmare was this?

He backed away from her, shaking his head, pushing with empty hands to keep her away. Ella? Or Janet?

A hand on his shoulder roused him. "Calum! Ye're dreaming. Wake up. Calum, wake up!"

The lad charged with tending him was bent over him, hands on his shoulders, holding him down while he shouted at him. He recognized the lad's voice.

"I'm awake."

Immediately, the lad let go of him and stepped back. "Ye were having a bad dream. Ye started moving, tossing yer head from side to side. Mhairi willna be happy to hear about that."

God's bones, had he destroyed all the work she'd done, the care they'd taken to keep his head still, all his time lying in this damned bed, only to ruin his injured eye during a bad dream?

"Fetch her, lad."

"I will."

Calum heard him move away. The chamber door opened and closed.

He was alone. Blessedly, silently, peacefully alone. No

one watching him. No one tending him. But for how long? Mhairi would come quickly, he knew. He took a deep breath, trying to soak in the peace. The sense of himself as he used to be, when he could see. Confident in himself and his abilities.

Would Janet come in Mhairi's place? That thought brought the nightmare crashing back. He'd dreamed of Ella and Janet and Marjorie. Because Marjorie lied to him? Because he feared Ella was lying to him, too? Was that the message of his dream? Three women, or two, and their lies? He pursed his lips, his peace broken. Until these bandages came off, he would never know.

CHAPTER 3

15 AUGUST, 1411

*E*lla led Calum along the path through the nearly empty bailey, gravel crunching under their boots. With most of the keep's residents either inside preparing the great hall for the Marymas feast, or out of the keep taking part in family celebrations or hunting, the healer approved coming outside if she didn't take him far and was careful. To Ella, the brilliant afternoon sunshine seemed an odd counterpoint to the darkness Calum had lived in for three sennights. Though he couldn't see it, she hoped the change in his surroundings, the warmth of the sun, and the fresh air would help speed his recovery.

"We're near the stables," he suddenly remarked, lifting his head in its direction. "I smell horses and their feed."

Startled, Ella nodded, then remembered to speak in Janet's low, clipped tones. Calum had suffered ringing in his ears since the battle. Just before they came outside, the healer removed the packing from them that muffled sound, worrying Ella. She had relied on it to help alter her voice, but the healer insisted it was time for it to come out as he had stopped complaining about the noise in his head. "Aye, we are," she answered. "What else do ye smell?" She hoped the onions in her pocket continued to mask her own scent. Likely he'd gotten used to the onion scent around her and knew she wasn't asking about herself. She hoped by the time they ended this deception, her clothes would not be permanently stained with the scent.

"Something acrid…woodsmoke and…metal. Hot metal," Calum told her. "The blacksmith's forge."

"We're approaching it. How did ye ken?" The forge was still, lacking on this feast day the clang of the smith's hammer on his anvil. The healer also agreed to this foray because the bailey would be more quiet than usual. She wanted to know if Calum's hearing had truly improved or if he'd simply learned to ignore the ringing.

Calum remained silent for a few moments as they walked farther. "My life depends on what I notice around me," he told her. "The iron has a tang that I taste as well as smell…and I felt the heat from the banked forge as we neared it."

"I did no'," she told him. What else did he notice that she failed to discern?

"I've lived in this keep most of my life," he added. "I can find my way around this bailey blindfold…" He stopped suddenly, stiffened and sucked in a breath.

Ella laid her free hand on her heart, pity for him welling up at his words. He would hear it in her voice, so she took a breath and tried encouragement. "Aye, ye can, Calum, very well. Yer senses are undimmed by yer time indoors."

"I am…I was a Brodie scout," he said, turning his face aside as though staring off into space while recalling the battle that made him an invalid these past weeks. "One of the best. What am I, if I can nay longer be what I was?"

Ella wanted to hug him, but a servant like Janet would never dare do so. Even to reassure him would be a risk for Janet. Some men would think nothing of forcing a servant they fancied to lie with them. She was certain Calum was not one of those men. Still, she saw nothing good in tempting him. But it didn't matter. She had no answer to give him.

If he wasn't acting out in frustration over his enforced blindness, he fretted over his future, his place in the clan. How he would fight if the battle they'd fought at Harlaw was repeated elsewhere. She reached for something to lighten his mood. "Ye need no' think to become a bard—ye dinna have the voice for it," she told him in a teasing tone. As soon as she said the words, she regretted them. Would Calum realize Janet had never seen him drunk and singing drinking songs with other men, but Ella had?

His brow furrowed, telling her she had his attention. Calum's lips tightened, then twisted, one side quirking up in what appeared to be a hard-fought attempt at a smile.

Relieved he didn't seem to have made the connection, Ella couldn't help smiling back. If his sense of humor was returning, he truly was getting better. He'd always had a light touch with his best friend Euan's gruffness. She'd missed it since he'd been injured.

Then his hands curled into fists. "If ye dinna take this wrapping from around my head, I'll do it myself. I canna bear this darkness any longer."

She stepped in front of him, grabbed his wrists and held them down by his sides, using her weight against his strength. She had not been this close to him, face to face, body to body, since he'd been injured, and the heat and scent of him distracted her for a moment. As many times as she discouraged his teasing advances before Harlaw, she found she now wanted him this close—even closer. But not like this. "Ye will no'!" She knew he could break her grip with little effort, but she had to prevent him. "The healer said yer eyes must remain covered—both of them—if ye wish to regain yer sight."

"What sight?" he snarled. "She is blinding me as surely as that shattered sword did."

Ella hoped he never said that in Mhairi's hearing. She would be hurt. "A steel splinter went into yer left eye. She told ye, what one eye does, they both do, so to let yer wound heal, ye canna try to use the other." Ella released his wrists and placed a hand on his arm, still heavily muscled despite his forced inactivity. "Ye were out of yer head with fever for days—"

"What? The healer said 'twas mild."

"She sought to reassure ye. She's treating yer eye with a tincture of wine, honey, and herbs that keep it from festering. And the fever is gone. So ye think all else is healed as well. But until the healer gives ye leave, 'tis too soon. Do ye truly wish to lose the sight in that eye?"

Calum was silent for a long moment before his shoulders dropped. "No' if I havena already," he bit out, defeated. "A blind scout is worthless, and a half-blind man fares little better. If I am to be useful as a warrior..."

"Ye have been so patient," she said, cutting him off, and risking much being so forward with him. She wished she could do as he asked and reveal his gaze. She missed the way he looked at her. The longing for her he hadn't hid— and now that she thought back on it, he never tried to disguise. But she heard the fear in his voice he struggled to keep inside. How he must long for the sight of blue skies... and everything else. As much as she wanted to soften her tone, with him, she had to be Janet, so she grated out, "Ye can tolerate waiting a wee more."

He pressed his full lips together, then spoke. "If at the end, the reward is being able to see ye."

The abrupt end to his sentence made Ella study his face —as much as she could see for the bandages. Was he teasing, or did he mean it? She couldn't tell by his tone of voice if he had become soft on Janet or knew her to be Ella. He sounded more like the old Calum—before he was injured. Less angry, if only a little. But his posture was still stiff.

Once the healer removed the bandages from his eyes, how would seeing her again as Ella affect him? How angry would he be to know she was Janet? She might have much to regret. Such as the tension in his jaw that told her she'd only added to his misery today. "I am sorry. I did no' mean to make ye feel worse."

"I ken it, lass," he said after a hesitation that put her even more on edge. "Thank ye for talking sense to me when all I want to do is something rash. 'Tis no' yer fault the Lowlanders fight with poorly forged blades."

She encouraged him to move with a light tug on his sleeve. "Ye were unlucky to be so near to one that shattered," she said as they walked along. "But," she added as his fists clenched yet again, "ye were lucky to have made it home from the battle so quickly, and to be under the care of the Brodie healer. That blow to yer head…Mhairi saved yer life. She may well have saved yer sight. I hope so."

"No' half so much as I."

She wanted to give herself—give Ella—credit for helping Mhairi, but she didn't dare mention that name. Janet had already been overly familiar for her station. Instead, she squeezed his forearm in sympathy. "We need to go in soon." She hesitated, then deliberately brightened her tone. "The Marymas feast is taking place this eve. Everyone is expected to attend. Ye, too." How she wanted him to be able to enjoy the celebration, to spend time with his friends, to laugh. It would be so good for him. She tensed, waiting for his response.

"Marymas? Already? How long have I been confined to that chamber?"

Ella sighed and walked on. He kept pace with her easily, despite the uneven ground. "Only a fortnight and a few days, Calum."

"So I'm to attend a feast I canna see and make a fool of myself trying to eat it?"

"I will be there to help ye."

He stopped again, head tilted back, face to the sky. If

he'd been facing the sun, she would have thought he sought its heat, or its strength. But they faced shadows.

Whether in frustration or despair, behind the bandages, his eyes were probably squeezed shut. She could only imagine what kind of battle must be raging inside this proud man. She dared not leave him standing here to brood. She could see his mood darkening with every moment that passed, his whole body stiff and his hands again curled into fists at his side. She had to do something to break the spell.

"Calum!" As Janet, she felt free to say his name more sharply than Ella ever would. "I've much to do before this eve. Will ye take me inside, please?" If his sense of humor failed, his sense of duty rarely did.

He took a breath, and it seemed his whole body deflated and shrank. His fists uncurled last, and he turned toward her. Slowly. "Aye."

She had made certain her hands retained enough calluses for him to feel them, so she took one of his strong hands in both of hers and turned him back the way they'd come. She had no doubt he would notice the roughness of her touch, and released him as quickly as she could. Relieved that he was moving, Ella guided him with a light touch on his arm toward the keep's main door.

Then her foot slipped on a patch of mud. She cried out and flailed, trying to catch herself, but before she fell to the ground, Calum scooped her up. He held her against his chest, his arms solid supports across her back and behind her knees. Sudden heat coursed through her, whether from Calum's body or her own embarrassment, she couldn't say.

"Are ye hurt…Janet?"

Heart pounding, she shook her head before remembering to speak. "Thanks to ye, Calum, nay. Ye saved me from falling. How did ye ken where I was?"

"I always ken where ye are." He started walking forward, still carrying her.

Ella shivered at the deep undertone of his voice rumbling through his chest and into her ribs, intensifying as the vibrations slipped deeper into her body. His words seemed to carry a promise she hoped for, but dared not name. If he paid such close attention to her, it must mean something.

But nay! Thanks to her altered voice and scent, he thought she was Janet, not Ella. How true were his feelings for her if he spoke so of Janet? Of a woman who smelled of onions! He always knew where she was? Why would he give a servant that sort of attention? Why would he admit it?

She thought he desired her and her alone, yet it seemed he was no better than any of the past men in her life. Faithless. She'd learned that the hard way with Dermott. Even Thomas, who'd only brought her home and divorced her to save her life. Determined to have their way with any woman in reach. "Ye can put me down," she told him, guilt and anger stealing her enjoyment of his nearness. No one else would know the apprehension that filled her, but anyone could see them. She must look ridiculous, being rescued by a blind man, no matter how good it felt to be held secure in his arms. Even now, the quiet bailey was too public a place for such a display.

"Are ye certain ye can remain standing?"

His tone was teasing, once again reminding her of Calum's good-natured humor before his injury, but his touch betrayed his concern, his hand on her back stroking up and down. He meant to soothe her, she knew, but instead, his touch set her blood to singing. Yet, he was flirting with Janet, not her. She fought down the feelings his touch elicited and took a breath. "Long enough to get inside, aye." Where she would find more onions. Maybe some garlic. Or rotten meat. Anything to break the spell Janet seemed to have over him.

He stood her on her feet and took her arm without further comment, but with a frown that made her fear that he'd been affected by holding her, too. Needing a distraction, she hurried them up the steps to the keep's heavy door and let him pull it open. Once he closed it behind them, his shoulders slumped and she realized he dreaded being confined indoors yet again.

She led him to the entrance to the great hall and paused. There was no one nearby. No one to call her by her true name. She could remain Janet, at least for now. She didn't know what she would do if someone forgot their ruse and called her Ella. Admit to it, she supposed, and deal with Calum's reaction as she must.

"Take a breath," she told him. So soon after being in his arms, it might be a risk to emphasize his sense of smell, but the festival preparations should cover her scent. She needed to distract him. "Tell me what ye sense." His broad chest rose and fell, and watching him made her hungry to be held against it again. Even if only as Janet.

"People and hounds," he said, his fierce expression smoothing into enjoyment. "And for the Marymas, bannocks. Lots of them."

"And more?"

"The hearth fire burning, and..." He lifted his head, nostrils flaring while he took another breath.

He looked proud, strong and confident, despite the healer's bandages covering his eyes and wrapping around his dark head.

"Roasting meats, aye, and tarts from the kitchen," he announced.

"I canna smell the pies, but all the rest, aye."

"Ye said my senses are undimmed. And I told ye, I notice everything." He turned his face to her. "I ken that Ella has been in my chamber, no' ye."

Ella froze. Nay! How did he know that? She'd been careful to keep the healer's onions and herbs on her any time she tended him.

"I ken her scent. I told the healer I did not want her there."

Ella fought to speak normally in Janet's low tones. "Perhaps ye only imagined...or something of her scent remains in the room from before the healer called the lads and me to ye."

Without the bandages over his eyes, she expected his gaze would be locked with hers. Was he trying to tell her he knew—or at least suspected—who she really was? Could he truly find her scent among all the others in the keep?

"Perhaps."

His acquiescence surprised her. She'd thought he would continue to challenge her. As he held her safe in his arms, he'd hesitated before calling her Janet. Was he playing with her? Mocking her? That, she would not tolerate. She'd been through too much, and learned too much, to be any man's plaything ever again.

But Janet wouldn't know to take offense. "If she has been in yer chamber, 'twas no' when I was present. And surely, she only meant to help ye." She summoned a chuckle. "What man would object to a beautiful lass caring for him?"

Calum's mouth thinned and his fists clenched. "What good is beauty to a blind man? Can ye tell me that?"

His words hit her like a dirk to the heart. Was that all she meant to him? He saw only her beauty? Even after the last year, he did not have a sense of who she was inside? He wouldn't feel the same about her if he couldn't see her ever again? She knew better. She'd spent enough time with him in the year since she'd come to Brodie to know he would have become bored with her very quickly if all she was to him was someone pleasant to look at. They'd had too many conversations. He knew her history and all she had suffered. How she looked should be the least thing about her that he cared for.

Nay, she would not accept that his enjoyment of her beauty was all she was to him. His fear and frustration sent those resentful words spewing from his mouth.

He pursued her from the moment he met her. He cared for her. He made his feelings for her evident without words, even if she didn't want to recognize them at the time. Instead, she held him off, certain that she was not ready to be close to any man, even one who interested her, and who pursued her as consistently as Calum did.

Why did every man think her beauty was all she had to offer? She thought Calum was better than that. She was sick of being wanted only for her face. It was the reason Thomas Ross immediately claimed her from among the three captured Munro lasses, but she showed him she had more spine in her than he expected. She escaped. It wasn't her fault her own Munro chief forced her to return to Ross with the husband she didn't want when Thomas came to reclaim her. Only her own strength in refusing food for weeks saved her, convincing Thomas that she would rather die than remain wed to him. At least then, he had done the honorable thing, brought her home to Munro and divorced her.

She thought Calum was different.

But was he? He treated Janet with as much courtesy—or more—than he'd given Ella lately. Did he really feel any affection for her, or did he treat any woman as well as he'd treated her in the past, and Janet now? Perhaps what she thought was his patience with her reluctance to get closer to him or to any man wasn't patience, but some sort of friendly indifference. Maybe she'd imagined he wanted her —after all, he'd never actually said as much.

Perhaps it was time to end this pretense. To remove this false face she wore around him, and to make him tell her the truth of how he felt about her. She wanted to tell him who she was, but the great hall was no place for such a conversation. For such a confrontation, if that was what it would become.

And if she was wrong about ending her deception right now, she could not let him fall in love with Janet. It would hurt her too much. She knew that was selfish. She'd ignored his advances again and again, but she'd learned, when she feared she'd lost him to his injuries, that she couldn't bear to be without him. He might be angry at her for what she'd done, but the Calum she knew would soon get past it.

Or would he? After succumbing to such a terrible injury, was he still the Calum she knew?

Who would Calum become if, as he feared, he'd lost half his sight? If he could not be the warrior he was before Harlaw? Would he still be the man she could love? Friends warned her he might be changed. Different. But she believed, deep inside, he would be the same man he'd always been, and he would adjust. Iain would give him every opportunity to assume an important place in the clan, no matter what. She would help.

So she must wait until the healer determined it was time to reveal his eye—and his future. The Marymas feast was a time to celebrate the Assumption, the coming harvest, and to prepare for the long winter ahead. It was also a celebration of good fortune. Of miracles. Ella hoped for two—that the feelings Calum once held in his heart for her remained, and that once his eyes were no longer covered, he would see on her face and in her eyes, the feelings for him that she had hidden from him for too long.

CALUM TOOK ANOTHER BREATH, annoyed when his belly rumbled in reaction to the scents of the feast being prepared. "I will return to my chamber now," he announced, not even certain Janet remained with him. She'd been silent since his angry comment.

"I'll take ye." Her voice had taken on a gruff edge. Had he hurt her feelings? He would never deliberately do such a thing to any lass. Or he wouldn't have, before Harlaw.

How much had this injury changed him? Calum knew he should be grateful he was still alive. Yet, he didn't know how much longer he could stand living like this. The enforced blindness was bad enough, but worse were these feelings for a woman who was not Ella. So like her in some ways, but not in ways he could be certain were real or contrived.

If Ella was indeed pretending to be Janet, he didn't know what he would do.

Was she? There were times he was convinced Ella attended him. At times, the onions Janet favored failed to completely mask her natural scent. But her touch seemed like that of a lass who worked with her hands, rougher than Ella's. Her voice was different, deeper, but not remarkably so.

Altered. Deliberately?

He'd held this woman in his arms moments ago, more closely than he'd ever been able to hold Ella. He'd nestled her body against his chest, her heat warming his hands, his arms, his blood. Surely, he could not be this attracted to any other woman but his Ella. He was a warrior. A scout. And Ella was the woman he loved. The one that he wanted for his wife. The woman he wanted to bed, damn it. Without any doubt, he should know the difference between them. Were his senses failing him? Or, after the blow to his head, was his mind?

Or was Janet a mummery cooked up between Mhairi and Ella to find a way around his wish that she not be involved in his care?

He could not bear for Ella to see him as weak and helpless, like a child. But, when he told Mhairi to keep her away from him, he might have been days too late to prevent it. She was at his bedside when he woke up. Had she cared for him until he regained his senses and objected? Had she cared for him as a mother cares for a sick wean? He couldn't stomach the idea of it.

He wanted to erase from her memory the misery of her forced marriage to Thomas Ross. He wanted to show her what love could be when it was right. What loving him could do for her. For both of them. Yet, how was he to arouse her to accept him as a man if she'd cared for him for days while he was unconscious and helpless?

A sudden sense of guilt further soured his belly. Had she damaged her hands to make the ruse more believable?

And what harm had he just done by his angry words? *What good was beauty to a blind man*, indeed? Yes, Ella was beautiful, but he loved all of her, not only her appearance. Her beauty encompassed who she was, how she cared for others—even for him, perhaps—and how she fought for and protected herself and her friends at Ross.

Yet, he'd told the truth. His angry outburst expressed his torment over the future he foresaw if he didn't get his sight back. If he lost his eye, he'd lose his place in the clan. Then, he'd have to give her up, too. She deserved to be with someone who could protect her. The thought tore at his guts. He wanted her, but only if he remained the man he once was—with both eyes.

He had to keep his distance until he knew who he would be, the warrior or the half-blind man.

He was confused, and he knew it. And tired from the walk outside, which added to the anger he struggled to control. How could he fight for his clan if a walk around the bailey exhausted him?

He felt a slight movement, as if Janet shifted her weight from foot to foot. She was waiting for him to answer her. "Nay, ye needna take me to my own chamber. Stay and enjoy the feast. I can find my way."

"Third door—"

"On the right. I ken it." He moved away without another word. He was at a loss for how to deal with Janet...or Ella...at this time. The healer must take these bandages from his eyes. Then, the deception he feared they practiced would be impossible. And he would know whether he had two good eyes and the future he had worked for his entire life, or if he would be forgotten among the clan's crippled and ill, struggling to find a way to make use of any skills he retained.

It was a grim thought, and soured his mood further. He needed to *see*! But after Janet's admonition, he retained enough sense not to rip the bandages from his head and eyes himself.

Where was the healer?

He stood still for a moment, orienting himself to the increase in sounds and movement around him as preparations for the feast got underway in the great hall. Had he gotten turned around? Which way should he go? Ah, the great hall's hearth was ahead of him…there. The scent of burning wood was stronger in that direction. The way sound bounced around the hall, seeming farther away in the same direction, told him the shape of the room. The stairs were…there. Someone was clumping down in heavy boots. Which meant the herbal was to the left. He turned that way, going slowly so as to avoid barking his shins on a bench or tripping over a trestle table. People saw him coming, of course, and helped him avoid obstacles. He thanked them and moved on, embarrassed to be treated as one who could not take care of himself, even though he knew they meant their assistance as a kindness.

Could he face them with a warrior's pride once he could see again? Or worse, could he live among those who'd known him as a warrior when half his sight was gone forever? That would be harder to survive than any battle he'd fought up to now. He must be freed from this darkness before he went mad. If he wasn't there already.

The last helpful voice told him he'd reached the hallway he wanted. Once he'd successfully transited the great hall, getting to his objective was easy.

"Healer, are ye within?" He knew he'd come to the right place. The scents of herbs and flowers, added to the often acrid or odorous potions and poultices she was constantly making, assaulted his nose.

"Good day to ye," he heard her say. "Where is…Janet?"

Her hesitation gave him another reason to think Janet was Ella. He didn't let Mhairi's use of the name distract him. "I left her to find her friends to enjoy the feast, and came to find ye."

"Come in, then. There's a stool six paces ahead of ye to yer right hand. Have a seat and tell me what ye want."

"I want ye to remove these wrappings from my eyes," he said as he found the stool and settled one cheek on it, then slid over to sit on it fully. "It has been long enough."

"I'll be the judge of that."

He felt as much as heard the healer approach him. He fought to keep his voice calm and level as he told her, "If ye dinna remove them, I will. I've lived in darkness too long. I must ken what my future will be."

She stayed silent long enough that he began to sweat. Would she deny him?

"I will uncover yer eyes long enough to check the injured one," she said. "But ye must accept that if I dinna like what I see, I may have to cover it yet again."

"Please. Dinna do that." He couldn't believe he'd been reduced to begging, but that's what blind men did, was it not? Only he would not be blind, merely one-eyed, if the healing had not gone well.

"Turn toward my voice. Ye will keep yer eyes closed," she ordered as she clipped the binding around his head and unwound it.

The feel of cool air on the skin of his face that she'd

kept covered for weeks, except for brief periods when she changed the bandages, nearly undid him.

"Eyes closed," she reminded him, then removed the pad over his damaged eye. "I'm going to touch yer eyelid," she warned, slid a warm finger down from his eyebrow and pulled up the lid.

Brightness assaulted him, but he reveled in it.

"Hmmm. What do ye see?"

"Light. Brightness. How is it?"

She let go of his lid. "Keep it closed."

He was happy to comply, wincing against the sting of tears the sudden brightness elicited. But her failure to answer him made his gut tense.

She removed the pad from his other eye. "Verra well. Open them slowly," she ordered.

At first, the light was too much, though she'd taken care to face him toward a dark corner of the herbal and not looking toward the hearth or even any candle flames.

His eyes teared, but he blinked and cleared them. Slowly, things came into focus. Both eyes or just the good one? He closed that lid and found he could still make out objects in front of him with the healing eye. The relief that filled him was so profound that it made his chest heavy, his arms leaden weights he couldn't lift.

"I can see with the injured one." He turned to her where he'd last heard her voice. "I see ye. A little blurry—"

"That is to be expected." She pointed across the chamber. "Tell me what ye see on my table over there."

"Two pots, three piles of green herbs. Rose petals. Pink."

He turned back to her in time to see her expression lighten into a smile.

"Do ye still have pain?"

"Only a little." She meant in his eye. His hearing was sharper since she removed the wadding in his ears. The headaches he had continued to suffer were diminishing. He'd kept them from Mhairi, not knowing what foul-tasting potion she'd force on him if she knew he still had them.

"Good. I am not surprised the light seems strong now. Ye will adjust to it as yer vision clears."

"Ye are certain that it will," he said, his words heartfelt. He desperately wanted them to be true, to relieve the weight smothering him since he woke up blind in his own bed.

"I'm certain ye have a good chance, if ye do as I say."

A good chance was better than nothing. "I'll do the best I can."

"Calum."

Her tone held a warning, so he relented and nodded. But he had to know something else, too. "Now, tell me the truth before I have to see for myself," he demanded, but lowered his voice when her eyes widened. He was not here to frighten her, but he needed answers. "Ella and Janet are the same person," he declared softly. He didn't make it a question.

The healer's cheeks pinked, and she glanced aside. "Ye suspected so."

"I did, though not right away."

Her reluctance to answer told him everything he

needed to know. She had lied to him. So had Ella. Fury sparked, choking him. He fought it down. The anger twisting his gut told him no matter how much he condemned what they had done, he had allowed himself to be deceived. He hadn't believed what his senses told him. He couldn't accept what his mind knew to be true, or thought to be false. In some fashion, he'd known all along that Janet was Ella, so he could not be angry with them alone. Most of his ire he must direct at himself. And he didn't know what to do about any of it.

CHAPTER 4

$\mathcal{E}$lla watched Calum walk away from her and make his careful way across the great hall. He'd said he wanted to go to his chamber, but he wasn't headed in the right direction to get to the stairs. She feared he would meet with disaster—a fall or some other embarrassment—but she was filled with pride that he would attempt it. Others helped him avoid hazards with a word or two. Those he accepted with more grace than she thought he would be able to summon, especially after the conversation they'd just had.

She stood by a table where some lasses sat eating and talking while they worked. Instead of taking a seat and helping them create the flower garlands that would decorate the tables for the feast, she could not take her gaze from him. Outside, walking in the bailey, he hadn't boasted when he said his other senses were still sharp. His determination and adaptability continued to impress her. Until she realized where he was headed. The hair lifted on the back of her neck. Not toward the stairs. He was going to Mhairi!

He'd meant it when he said he could not stand to remain in the dark any longer. He intended to beard the healer in her own den. She prayed Mhairi did not admit the Janet ruse. If she did, what would Calum do about it? Accept that she'd done everything she could to take care of him, including lie to him? Or reject her for her subterfuge?

She gripped the end of the table hard enough to whiten her knuckles, torn between the urge to run after him and feeling frozen in place.

If only his eye healed well enough to let him understand that he had not lost the future he'd expected to have. That he would still be a warrior for the clan. A man in the way he understood manhood. Perhaps then, he would forgive her.

If he lost the eye, could he adapt to that? She hoped he never had to find out.

She couldn't sit here waiting for the axe to fall. Without a word, she forced her feet to move, left the table, and followed Calum's path across the hall. She waited silently by the door while the healer removed his coverings, and rejoiced at the vision he described. *He could see.*

Her mind spun with how to remove Janet from his life and become Ella once again. She didn't have much time. She needed to wash the onion scent from her hands and breath before he saw her. And perhaps some more of the healer's cream would finish softening the damage the lye did to her hands. She started to back away from the door but her boot scraped on the flagstones.

Calum turned at the sound, this time with his eyes open. "Ella. I see ye."

She was out of time.

She went to him, hands out to grasp his if he raised them, or to give him a hug full of joy and relief. "I'm so glad ye do," she said when he let her capture his fingers. Then his brusque tone sank in. "Is aught amiss?"

He lifted her hands and sniffed, then turned one over and thumbed her palm before he pulled his fingers free. "Will ye remain Ella now? I smell Janet about ye." When his brow lowered and he glanced again at her hand, she realized he knew about their deception.

Ella's body chilled as if she'd plunged into a frigid loch. She glanced at the older woman, who shook her head, her lips pursed with regret.

She had no choice. If she dreamed of having any future with this man, she must admit what she'd done and hope he understood why she'd done it.

"Calum, I couldna bear to see ye suffering," she began. "I helped Mhairi care for ye before ye woke up. We...I... created Janet so that ye would allow me to remain at yer side, where I needed to be. Where I thought I belonged."

"Did ye think so? Ye lied to me."

How could his newly revealed visage be so full of censure? How dare he condemn her for tending to him when he could not attend to himself!

"I did everything to help you heal. And to help you see again. If ye canna forgive that—"

"Ye believed I would thank ye for going against my

wishes and seeing me as helpless as a bairn." The chilly, flat tone matched the frost in his gaze.

Ella crossed her arms and wrapped her hands around them for warmth and protection. "Like ye are behaving now?" She shook her head as he stood. To make her look up at him? To intimidate her? Had he forgotten she was made of stronger stuff than that? "I never saw ye as a bairn." She stiffened her spine, and met his gaze. "I care too much for ye to ever treat ye as a wean."

"If ye truly did, ye wouldna have tried to fool me. Playing such games with a blind man was a kind of torture. Losing my sight wasna enough for ye? Ye had to make me fear I was losing my senses and my mind as well with yer deception?"

Cold skittered down Ella's spine. Had she done that? She thought back to his first day out of the keep when they walked in the bailey. He'd been so proud of his ability to notice and identify everything around him. She hadn't realized it at the time, but he'd made it clear his mind was his greatest weapon, using what his senses told him to make his way around the bailey he could not see, but he could sense. And without meaning to, she made him doubt both his senses and what he thought about the things he noticed, the map he'd built in his mind of where he was in relation to the world around him. If she'd weakened him as a warrior and a scout, she'd done more damage than either she or Mhairi could have imagined.

"Calum," the healer interjected, "Ella helped me care for ye as she has done for others, as ye well ken. There is nay shame in that. She lied to protect ye, and that is the only reason. Dinna blame her, for I went along with the ruse. I helped her craft it. Blame me for not having a better answer to the question of how to keep ye safe while ye healed."

"Ye helped her damage her hands?" Calum studied the older woman for a long moment. "And after that, I am supposed to trust her? Or ye?"

"Her hands will heal. Ye dinna think that by going to such lengths to help ye, despite yerself, she proved her loyalty to ye?"

He huffed out a breath. "Am I free to go?"

Ella's heart twisted in her chest. He'd refused to answer. Refused to acknowledge that there was anything good in what she'd done.

Mhairi paused, frowning. "I must cover the injured eye again so ye dinna rub it and do more damage to it while ye sleep."

"Nay."

"*Wheesht!*" Mhairi's irritation showed in that one word, telling Calum his stubbornness wasn't appreciated.

Ella felt a small surge of satisfaction.

"I willna cover both. 'Tis time for ye to start using both yer eyes again. Ye can uncover it in the morning. We'll do the same for the next sennight. After that, yer eye should be healed well enough that ye may sleep without protecting it. And yer vision should continue to improve."

He sat back on the stool without another objection and let Mhairi tend him while Ella watched. She felt frozen to the floor, unable to move, either to go to him or to leave. When the healer finished, he stood and walked out of the herbal without another glance or word to either of them. But she noticed he stayed to the right side of the doorway, even laying a hand on the stone as if to steady himself. Of course, with his left eye covered, he was blind on that side. He'd favor what he saw to his right. Being half blind, he'd said, also worried him. Now he knew what it would be like. It had to be another frustration to add to all the others he'd suffered since Harlaw.

Ella sank onto the stool Calum vacated. "He willna forgive me." She kept her tone matter-of-fact, but inside, her heart was in pieces. Sharp, jagged little pieces that cut with every breath she took. If this was going to be their future—if she made such an effort and he reacted like he'd rather die than accept her help—she'd been wrong about him. "Am I never to find a man who accepts me—all of me —for who I am?"

The healer pressed her lips together and raised a finger. "Dinna let him belittle ye. Without ye, he might no' have regained his sight. I couldna be there all the time. Ye kept his head still and helped him when he was desperate to move and risked his sight out of frustration."

"I dinna think he will believe that. Ye are the healer. I am...nothing but a bonnie lass."

"Perhaps as his eyesight clears and he regains his confidence, he will accept the part ye played in his recovery. He is still hurt and embarrassed by it all, but that will pass."

"Will it? Will he come to me and beg my forgiveness? After this, I canna...I willna go to him." Or any other man at all. If she couldn't break down the walls Calum built against her, if nothing worked with him, she would give up and accept that she was cursed with bad luck in matters of the heart.

The healer nodded, closing her eyes briefly, then captured Ella's gaze with her own. "If he doesna, there is yer answer. Ye have been strong for him, but ye must be stronger still for yerself. He will come to ye, or ye will tire of waiting and find what ye seek in another man."

"I dinna want another," Ella said, turning to stare out the doorway Calum had exited, the pieces of her heart a leaden weight in the bottom of her chest. "I thought I'd found what I needed in him. I hope that I still can. And that he will come to see I did the best I could for him. If he will let me, I will fight for him—for us. But if I must," she vowed, "I will find my way forward without him—or any other man at all."

CALUM SQUINTED against the brilliant shaft of sunlight that suddenly lit the Moray Firth and turned it into a restless silvery bonfire. At first, heavy clouds made the light bearable for his initial foray outside without an eye covering. But no longer. The wind was rising, tearing the low clouds apart, making ragged edges that let sunlight glow. Reflections flashed in the agitated water's surface.

The healer had finally removed the last bandage yesterday, giving him back the depth perception he'd sorely missed and a blurry but useful return to vision on his left side. Still, he struggled to focus on the target set up against the outside wall of the keep. His eyes were still sensitive to bright light, making the injured one fill with tears and sting. He lowered his longbow and wiped away the wetness on his cheek with the back of his left hand.

Mhairi had warned him not to touch his eye and ruin all her work and his hard-fought patience. On pain of death, she'd scolded. And she would make it a painful death, he was certain she knew how. So he let the eye leak and fought the urge to rub it. She'd warned it might do this for days or weeks to come, and he must let it be.

Let it be. Like he did everything in his life now. Including Ella. She was avoiding him. Or he was avoiding her. He wasn't certain which was more true. Perhaps both. She'd lied to him. And he'd hurt her. Badly. The healer was not happy about that and never missed an opportunity to remind him that what Ella did showed how much she cared about him. For him. And that she deserved his forgiveness. The last time she lectured him, he warned the healer to cease bringing it up or he would stop coming to her.

"Just try it, laddie," she'd scoffed. "Ye must be careful for sennights more, or the thing ye fear most could still come to pass."

The thing he feared most? Losing his sight in one eye? Or losing Ella? He'd already done that. Or as near as could be. Both possibilities seemed to have changed his life for the worse. And the only one he could control was not rubbing his damned eye, even when any stab of bright light made tears run down his face like he was a *greeting wean*. He'd accused Ella of thinking of him as a bairn. Now, except for his size, he must look like one. With his tears, all that was missing was a wean's wailing, and God's bones, he remembered times when he'd been tempted to give in to the urge to cry out in his despair.

He missed his friendship with Ella, but he couldn't find a way to let go of his anger. What would it take for him to forgive her? He didn't know how to fix any of this.

Perhaps Euan was right. Ella lied to him because he was being an arse then, just as he was now. But she, as Janet, also tried to tell him that his skills as a scout were his way forward. When she'd taken him outside, even blindfolded, he'd still been able to identify where he was in the bailey and what was around him. And where she was when she slipped, close enough to scoop her up into his arms. The onions hadn't been what made him aware of her presence. It was her. Ella. She had tried to prove to him that he was enough, his senses were undimmed, and he could still thrive. He never should have doubted that she would go to any lengths to care for him. Even to act against his wishes.

Disgusted with himself, he dropped the bow and his arrows on the ground and stalked toward the seaside cliff. The firth danced and shimmered in the changeable light. In the past, he might have admired the beauty of the display, but today it only served to add to his anger and frustration. He could see, damn it. Not perfectly. Not as well as he used to. But well enough on a cloudy day. He lifted his gaze to the ragged sky, then turned quickly away as another spear of light pierced his eye. And his temper. Damn it! Days more of this he might be able to abide, but sennights? Months? And what if it never stopped? What good would he be then?

Footsteps sounded behind him. He recognized Euan's tread and stiffened.

"The clouds are starting to clear," his friend announced as if it wasn't immediately apparent to anyone who bothered to look. "If yer eye is paining ye, we can do this in the gloaming later today."

Calum tensed, all but overcome with the urge to whirl and hit something, but the only target was Euan, and he didn't deserve Calum's ire.

Instead, he heaved a breath and nodded but didn't turn to face his friend. "Go on in. I'll follow ye shortly."

Euan knew his temper better than to question him. Calum imagined he stared, then nodded before turning away to gather bows and arrows. He'd leave the target in place for after sunset, when they'd try again.

As much as Calum hated the necessity, he'd never survive a battle unless he learned to compensate for his vision. He should be thanking Euan, as the Brodie arms master and as his friend, for standing with him, rather than fighting the urge to pummel him into the ground.

He stayed where he was until he no longer heard his friend, then he turned back to the wall. The target was still in place. They would return later. Euan meant what he'd promised. He always did.

Something moved and Calum lifted his gaze. Shocked, he took a step back when he spotted Ella looking down at him, then realized his peril so near the cliff's edge. He straightened and moved forward to safety as he studied her. Thank the saints he hadn't been standing on the edge of the cliff or he would have gone over. Her hair blew in the breeze. She clutched the shawl around her shoulders together in one hand, the other lay over her mouth, her expression unreadable. No, not that. Controlled. Sad and fighting not to show it.

Terrified by his near plunge over the cliff? Or pitying him?

That, he could not abide. With an oath, he strode away, around the curve of the palisade to the wall's gates and through. He headed straight for the keep's heavy oak door, never looking to see if Ella still stood on the rampart. He didn't want to know.

Why was she up there? Had Euan told her he would be helping Calum outside? He couldn't believe Ella still wanted to watch over him. But surely she wasn't there by chance.

It made no sense. Why would a woman want a mate who was so weakened? Was that why she went against his wishes? Because she treated him like anyone ill or injured, doing for them what they needed, and not what they wanted? Had he misread her all along?

His memory of her expression stabbed at him every time he recalled it. How dare she pity him.

When Ella heard Euan was taking Calum outside for his first attempt at archery since he'd been injured, she hurried to the wall walk to find them. Clouds that threatened rain all day were starting to thin, and she wondered how much stronger sunlight would affect him. But when she saw

Calum outside, bow in hand, a sheaf of arrows on his back, her worries fled. He seemed comfortable. Even focused as he studied the target Euan set up.

He was making great strides. The healer had finally removed the covering from his eye and warned him to be careful or she'd have to put it back. Ella was certain that threat would make him take care of his eye. And if he didn't, well, the healer's tincture had served him well so far. She hoped it would continue to ensure his eye healed completely and well.

Target practice would help him adjust to the changes in his vision. It was something he'd done since he was a lad. The technique, the movements, should be second nature to him. All but instinctive.

So why did he hesitate?

He grimaced as sunlight lanced through a break in the thinning clouds, and her heart dropped as he swiped at his cheek below his left eye. She wanted to call out to him to be careful, but knew that would only make his frustration worse. After he and Euan exchanged a few words, Euan picked up their weapons and left Calum near the cliff's precipice, staring out over the firth. It would embarrass him to know she was watching him like a mother watches a wean. Without thinking, she lifted a hand to cover her mouth. A mistake. She'd done it as he turned back toward the wall. The movement attracted his attention, and he saw her. His quick recoil took him a step closer to the cliff's edge. She blanched, her breath frozen in her throat until he took a few steps forward, away from certain death. He'd nearly fallen. If he had gone over, it would have been her fault. She dropped her hand to her heart and did her best to alter her expression into a neutral one, but he was already walking to the gate, no longer looking at her.

She leaned her forehead against the cold stone, berating herself for even being up here. Being seen. He must have recognized the dismay in her eyes. She'd made things worse for him, which was not at all what she'd intended to do. Indulging her curiosity led to this and probably deepened the rift between them.

She was a fool.

BOTH EUAN and Kenneth showed up at his chamber door after the supper hour, a meal he'd skipped while he sought solitude to nurse his foul mood. As tempted as he was to tell them to go away, Calum knew he wouldn't be able to deny them.

"I told ye we'd try again in the gloaming. Ye'd best come now before we lose the light altogether," Euan said.

Kenneth stood at his back carrying their weapons and sheaths of arrows.

"Ye brought Kenneth so he would ken how poorly I shoot, is that it?"

"What? Nay!"

Kenneth covered up Euan's irritated sputter with a statement of his own. "I heard at supper, where ye were missed, that ye two planned to do this, and I decided to join ye. Ye are no' the only one who needs some low light practice, aye?"

"Aye, right." Calum frowned but accepted Kenneth's explanation. It sounded like something he'd do. He tried a small smile to make up for his reaction to Kenneth's presence. "Let's go, then."

Outside, Calum looked first to the ramparts, to see if Ella dared to be up there again. He had not wanted her watching over him when he was confined to his bed, and he didn't need her doing it now. And it would be so much worse for Kenneth and Euan to notice her there. Thankfully, the only person he saw was a guard standing a good distance from them, his back to them, as well. Relieved, Calum dropped his gaze and found that someone, probably Kenneth, had set up extra targets.

Without debate, each of them moved into position on one and nocked an arrow. Tension made Calum's muscles tight. Could he do this with Iain's tanist and the arms master watching? He was used to hitting the bullseye consistently. But now, he might miss the target completely. Nay. He would not. He took a breath, pulled and let fly. The arrow hit solidly a few inches to the right of his usual spot, but all in all, it wasn't a bad shot.

He heard Euan's and Kenneth's arrows finding their targets, but didn't glance their way. They were both master archers. They wouldn't miss. And if they were shooting, they weren't watching him.

He nocked another arrow and lined up a little to the left of his last shot. It landed closer to center, but still not where it should be. He fired another and another, tracking nearer to his target each time as he learned how to adjust to the state of his vision. He experimented with aiming higher and lower to see if that had any effect. Closing his left eye and depending on his right eye made him miss even farther to the right than his first attempt. It wasn't perfect, but the left eye was helping.

With every shot he learned something, and the weight of his fears for his future eased a little. By the time he needed to retrieve his arrows, he felt if not happy, at least calmer.

Euan and Kenneth joined him before he did so.

"Good shooting," Euan said.

Kenneth nodded. "I see what ye did, trying different angles and tracking in to compensate for the difference in yer vision." He indicated the movement toward the center of Calum's first shots and the higher and lower ones that followed. "Excellent thinking, Calum. Ye came very close to yer usual skill. More practice should get ye where ye want to be."

Calum nodded, at a loss for what to say to Kenneth's praise. He'd succeeded better than he'd dared hope, and with Kenneth's approval, he could continue to refine his skill.

"We're losing the light," Euan remarked, "or I'd go another round. Tomorrow, then?"

"Aye," Calum agreed, eager after Kenneth's approval to do whatever it took to get better.

Kenneth nodded and went to collect the arrows from his target. Calum and Euan did the same, then they all went back inside the gates. Kenneth left them to put their weapons away, saying he'd join them inside.

"I call for an ale," Euan announced and gestured toward

a table in the great hall. "What ye just did should be celebrated."

"An ale wouldna go amiss," Calum agreed and moved forward to claim a spot.

Kenneth joined them as a serving lass brought their drinks.

Calum asked for some food to go with his, his belly having unknotted enough for him to be hungry. The lass gave him a smile and hurried away to fetch what was left from the supper he'd skipped.

They talked weapons and tactics, the conversation so comfortingly normal that it gave Calum as much hope as his successful archery practice earlier. When his food arrived, he fell to with more appetite than he'd had since he'd been injured. The lass brought extras for Kenneth and Euan, so they all chewed as they talked, and before long, several other men joined them.

"Calum, 'tis good to see ye among us again," one remarked. "Ye look well."

"Aye," another joined in. "I hope we'll see ye on the practice ground soon."

"Nay tomorrow," Kenneth cautioned. "Ye'll need the healer's blessing to fight with a blade or hand-to-hand."

Though it rankled, he knew Kenneth was right. He couldn't yet depend on his left-side vision to defend against an attack from that side. Archery was one thing. Swordplay could get him injured worse than the injury he'd already suffered. Or get him killed.

"I'm nay a fool," Calum told him. "I dinna need any of ye

lot taking my head from my shoulders because I canna clearly see ye coming."

"So yer vision is still no'…" the man trailed off as if unsure how to describe it.

Calum's improved mood allowed him to reply charitably. "Completely clear and sharp? Nay, 'tisna, but 'tis getting better. Ye'll have yer chance at me soon enough."

Euan lifted his cup. "I'll drink to that."

The men joined him with convivial laughter that warmed Calum down to his bones.

Conversation continued in a pleasant rumble around the table. Calum sipped his ale, simply enjoying his return to the life he'd feared he'd lost. Euan was in a debate with one of the other lads about the best source of steel for weapons, one arguing Spanish steel, another saying the French had good blades, but maybe they got them from the Spanish.

A little niggle of unease uncurled in Calum's belly. This was too close for comfort to the subject of the shattered sword that injured his eye. He forced his attention to the other side of the table where two of the lads were debating the merits of several of the serving lasses. Like most men, he enjoyed lasses, their company, their beauty, everything about them. He didn't need to compare them to appreciate them. Still, he preferred listening to what these lads liked about them over discussing the merits of swords.

Until one of the lads stumbled over a name certain to ruin Calum's good mood. "Janet…uh, Ella. Or Janet…"

Calum dropped his gaze to the tabletop and froze, not

wanting to be seen paying attention to what they were saying, but wanting to hear the rest of the sentence. He felt Kenneth shift beside him. So, Kenneth had heard it, too. Did everyone know about Ella's deception? Did they all think him a fool for not realizing from the first moment who Janet really was? Had everyone in the clan been lying to him?

Chuckles from that end of the table grated more than Calum could take. He stood and eyed the men. "What's so amusing?"

The men turned to each other, guilt written plainly on their faces. "Ah, a bad jest," one admitted.

"Why dinna ye share it with the rest of us, aye?" Calum goaded. He might as well find out what everyone really thought about him.

"Nay. 'Twasna that funny," the man's companion insisted.

"So, ye'll laugh behind my back, but no' tell me to my face, is that it?"

Kenneth reached up and put a hand on his arm. "Ye're making too much of this, Calum. Sit and finish yer ale."

Euan had risen to stand beside Calum when he first challenged the men. "They're *pished*, Calum. Dinna pay them any heed." He turned to the men in question. "The two of ye have had enough. Go on with ye to yer beds and sleep it off before ye cause any more trouble."

When it looked like they would argue, Kenneth rose, too. "Enough lads. Take Euan's advice before I have to make it an order."

The resistance on the two men's faces folded with

Kenneth's threat. They rose and walked away without further argument.

Both Kenneth and Euan turned to Calum and gestured him to take his seat.

"Finish yer ale," Euan said again.

Calum shook his head and stepped away from the table. "I've had enough as well. I'm for finding my bed."

Euan traded a look with Kenneth, then nodded. "Rest well, my friend. We'll practice more on the morrow."

Calum nodded and left them, his good mood fled, and the weight of all he'd been carrying firmly back on his shoulders. He could stomach a lot, even poor jests, but not their pity. Never that.

CHAPTER 5

Ella avoided the training ground for the next sennight. After Calum's reaction when he saw her watching him from the rampart, she dared not run into him there. It would bring back an uncomfortable memory for both of them. Did he know how close he'd come to the edge of the cliff when he saw her? She shuddered every time she thought of it.

She knew he'd been improving every day with bow and arrow. He'd moved inside the keep's walls from that private practice area Euan had set up for him outside, overlooking the firth. Her friends kept her informed about his progress, how his strength was returning, his aim improving and how he hoped soon to get permission from the healer to pick up a blade again.

All that was wonderful news. Ella was happy for him, truly. But she couldn't escape the sadness that filled her every time she thought of him. Nor the resentment for his repudiation of all she had done to help him, and how he rejected her.

The only time she saw him was at meals, like now. She shared her midday meal with Muireall, Annie, and her sister Cat, while Calum sat across the great hall with the other men. He'd been welcomed back into their company, at least by most. She'd heard about the dispute the night after he'd first picked up a bow. Men could be so thoughtless. So cruel. Even when they didn't mean to be. She hated to imagine the damage their callous jests had done to the progress Calum made that evening with Euan and Kenneth. The two jesters had apologized the next day, but Calum now knew her deception was widely known and supported. Even though she'd been nowhere nearby, once again she'd been the source of embarrassment for him.

"Ye are miles away, Ella," Muireall said, jostling her with an elbow to her side. "And I see what—or who—ye are trying so hard no' to look at. What are ye thinking, lass?"

It was impossible to keep her gaze from straying to Calum. She wished she'd never conspired with the healer. Instead, Ella should have let her do what Calum wanted and just let the lads tend him. She didn't know how to say the words to answer her friend's question. Had she truly acted for him, or only to satisfy her own wish to be needed by him? Despite male reactions to her appearance, she'd never thought of herself as excessively proud, but her pride had gotten the better of her, and left both of them with broken hearts.

"Perhaps it was for the best," she said on a sigh, then, when Muireall gave her a confused look, her brows drawn together, Ella explained. "Losing him. He kens I am damaged goods. He kens I was forced into a marriage with a man I didna ken and could never love." A man who used her for his own pleasure, and to improve his standing within his clan. She didn't know if she would ever be comfortable offering another man the intimacy he would want from a wife, not again. Not after how married life had been with Thomas Ross. He wasn't cruel. He was basically a kind man, but he tended to be indifferent to her needs. Her wishes. She couldn't say those words aloud. Instead, she said, "I thought Calum was different. Patient. Steadfast. He knew my story and did not blame me. Until now. Until I pushed too hard. And lied to him." She hadn't known how important honesty was to him. And how deeply he felt she'd betrayed him. She'd had no idea. While she clung to the illusion that Calum could get beyond her past and truly love her, she'd only fooled herself. With her Janet ruse, he'd seen the real woman, the one with faults and flaws, not just the beauty he admired or the lass he wanted to rescue from the Ross camp. And she didn't measure up.

"Ye didna lie...exactly," Annie broke in. "And eventually he'll realize that. Once his bruised ego recovers. *Men*," she huffed. "Those images they have of themselves are the most fragile part of them." She took a bite of her meal and chewed before she added, "'Tis a wonder we tolerate them at all."

"Ah, it sounds to me like Iain has done something..." Ella said, glad of the chance to change the subject.

"Nay, just a man being a man. He didna like a suggestion I made about something he considers a male prerogative."

"Men," her sister Cat snorted in solidarity.

The byplay gave Ella time to relax and she summoned a smile.

"That's better," Muireall said and patted her hand. "And by the way, as often as ye sneak looks at Calum, he's sneaking looks at ye. I wouldna be so certain he's over ye."

"For all the good 'twill do him," Annie added. "Ye are a strong woman, Ella. Make him crawl to ye. Dinna ye give in too easily."

Ella choked on the sip she'd taken while Annie spoke. Her words too closely echoed the vow Ella made to the healer the day Calum's sight revealed her face while she still wore Janet's scent and damaged hands. "I'll keep that in mind," she answered when she could speak again.

But would she? Truly, it probably didn't matter. Neither one of them seemed in a hurry to approach the other. To make amends. To find a way back to the path they'd been on. It might never happen. And never was a long time.

CALUM KNEW HE SHOULDN'T, but as he walked out of the great hall, he couldn't help glancing toward Ella. Fortunately, she was on his good side, so he didn't have to look directly at her to see her. His peripheral vision was sufficient on that side to see her with Annie, Cat, and Muireall, enjoying their meal and talking. About him? Probably, because Annie watched him with a distinct crease between her brows as he passed through the hall. He had no doubt that the lasses had decided he'd hurt their friend. There would be hell to pay at some point. Probably with no warning.

And probably with painful consequences. For him, and perhaps for their husbands for supporting him.

"Ach, ye'd best keep clear of Annie," Euan said from beside his left shoulder. "She's got a look that doesna bode well for ye."

"I ken it," he answered. Thoroughly in the clan's lady's bad graces was not a desirable place for anyone to be. "But there's naught I can do about it."

"Ye could stop treating Ella like a pariah."

Kenneth's advice stung.

Calum had been doing exactly that. "Is everyone against me on this? She lied to me. And everyone—*everyone*—kenned it but me, which means everyone has been lying to me. She made a fool of me." He held up a hand, too annoyed with them to admit he'd long suspected that Janet was Ella before the truth came out. "Nay, dinna say it. I've heard a thousand times how she only meant to help me."

"Then get that stick out of yer arse and give the lass a chance. She still watches ye. Sadly. And ye watch her the same way. Ye both are fools to let this go on."

They passed out of the great hall into the bailey and sunshine. Calum squinted against the sudden brightness.

"Ye are tolerating that better," Kenneth noted.

"A wee," Calum admitted, perversely grateful for the change of subject. Not that this one was any better. He was not well enough by far. His dream of fully regaining his vision, his abilities, and his place as a Brodie scout still seemed dangerously out of reach. For how much longer?

"Ye might treat the lass the same way," Euan said. "As a situation that can get better. If ye let it. Ye seemed happy with each other before ye were injured. Even if ye were friendly, but no' actually together, ye could at least be civil, and enjoy each other's company."

Calum stopped moving so quickly that Euan bumped into him from behind. Turning, Calum fixed him with a glare. "Enough. I've heard enough. I've had enough. Whether Ella and I ever speak to each other again—or anything else—is up to us and will happen or no' as we decide. Yer nagging doesna help matters."

Euan and Kenneth exchanged a grin, which was not at all the reaction Calum expected.

"*Ella and ye?*" Euan laughed in his face. "'Tis the first time I've heard ye mention the both of ye in the same sentence in weeks. Perhaps we're making a dent in that stubborn hide of yers."

"Aye?" Calum snorted. "Well, dinna believe it."

"Then perhaps ye'd rather we all head for the training ground and make a more physical dent in that stubborn hide of yers," Kenneth suggested.

"Ye ken I canna. Mhairi will have my hide if I pick up a blade."

"Archery it is. Ye did well on the nearer targets yesterday. 'Tis time to move them farther away and see if ye can still shoot straight."

⚓

MUIREALL TOOK ELLA ASIDE after the meal and after Annie left to deal with some problem she hadn't wanted to discuss, but which they both assumed had to do with Iain and something he wanted, or a bairn. Ella walked beside Muireall toward the door out of the keep, all the while thinking she'd never forget the day she took Calum outside, and he carried her back into the keep through that door, then went straight to the healer to get his bandages removed. It had been a disaster, and she should have expected it. She should not have followed him. All the bad feelings between them stemmed from that day.

Or had they? She couldn't shake the sense of guilt that told her he had a right to be angry, and that she'd done a foolish thing. And now, she had no idea how to fix it.

Cat moved outside with them, but mentioned visiting the seamstress and left them on their own.

"I want to talk to ye a wee longer," Muireall told Ella once they were alone. "Ye should ken I dinna entirely agree with what Annie told ye."

Ella frowned in confusion. "I dinna ken what ye mean."

"I think ye shouldna wait for Calum to crawl to ye. Annie doesna want to see ye hurt again, and I agree with her on that. But lass, Calum is a proud man, one who thinks ye betrayed him in some way that makes nay sense to us, but drives his anger. I believe some of the blame he places on ye is actually his reaction to what happened to him, but ye gave him a convenient target for it."

Ella nodded, despair swamping her. "I ken that. If I could go back and do it over—"

"But ye canna. Ye can only go forward. And forward is

through Calum's hurt feelings. Dinna let yer guilt stop ye. There is naught wrong with ye. Ye tried to help. It went wrong. Verra well, the current situation reeks. So change it. Dinna keep avoiding him. Go after what ye want."

Ella crossed her arms, her gaze on the floor between them. "What if I am nay certain what that is?" She thought she had been. Before Harlaw. But Calum after Harlaw was so changed, so angry and distant. She didn't blame him for what he felt, but she also no longer knew how to deal with him. She'd tried and this disaster was the result.

Muireall laughed, not amused, but mocking. "Keep telling yerself that and naught will change," she warned. "Ye ken exactly what—or who—ye want. And so does Calum. He chased ye around the Moray Firth for a reason. Remind him of that. Yer beauty entranced him. Dinna blush, ye ken 'tis true. Before he kenned aught about ye, he liked what he saw. Then he learned that ye are a caring and a good person, despite what he saw ye go through. He liked having your kindness directed at him. He enjoyed yer company, and the bond between ye two strengthened because of it."

"And then I broke it." How many times must she suffer that stab of regret that pierced her chest?

"Mayhap. Or mayhap ye were a convenient target for his fractured pride and his fury at what happened to him. Or his fear about how life in the clan will be different and perhaps less than he expected. He had an important position, but at the moment, he thinks he's lost it forever. The lads are helping him train to compensate for the changes. Mayhap ye can help him regain his pride."

Ella shook her head. "I embarrassed him. And the teasing embarrasses him even more. I'm doing the exact opposite of helping him regain his pride."

"The teasing will stop. Soon, I think. The lads tire of it and will find something else to amuse them."

"I hope so."

"Ye need a plan," Muireall told her. "We'll think of something. Ye canna go on as ye are. Nor can he."

"Nay, we canna. But a plan? To do what? Convince Calum that he was wrong and I was right? Ye can see how well he'd accept aught like that. He's no' a fool. He'll think I'm plotting again to get him to do something I want. If making him fall in love with me—or at least to be open to the possibility—was that easy, everyone would do it with the objects of their own affections."

"Ella, everyone does make the effort to make someone fall in love with them. 'Tis what happens when we fall in love. 'Tis part of learning about the other person, and letting him learn about ye. 'Tis hard work. It seems to me that Calum has forgotten much of what he kenned about ye before his injury."

"If the answer was to spend time together, we'd have been together long before now. As ye said, he chased me around the Moray Firth for a reason. I've been here a year, and we're no closer to a vow than we were when ye and I first got here. In fact, we're further apart than ever." She stared toward the keep's gate and the open sky beyond it. She might as well sprout wings and fly as to hope anything would change Calum's poor opinion of her at this point.

Muireall shook her head, her eyes flashing. "Ask him to

train ye as Iain is training other lasses. Ye'd spend time together and be close to each other. Very close."

Iain taught the lasses hand-to-hand fighting with dirks and smaller blades. They trained with wasters, the wooden swords used to begin training the youngest lads, then graduated to larger ones the older lads used before beginning to fight with dulled metal blades. Those would bruise, but were unlikely to break the skin, much less to remove any body parts.

Ella huffed. "Calum would never agree to an arrangement like that. And why would I ask him when I can work with Iain and the other lasses?"

"Because ye want to be with Calum, no' Iain, ye daft lass," Muireall told her.

"Wanting to be with him and wanting him to teach me how to fight are very different things, my friend."

"But with the same result. Proximity. Touching. Striving together. Doing something with him that he kens well, which lets him be manly and strong, aye?"

The more she thought about it, the more Muireall's suggestion made sense. "That may be, but I dinna think I can ask him. I'd be too embarrassed."

"What if ye didna have to ask him? What if ye go to train with Iain and he asks Calum to take ye on?"

"Get Iain involved in this scheme? Ach, nay. I'd rather ask Calum myself. At least then he can laugh at the idea and say nay to me without having to turn down Iain."

CHAPTER 6

Calum, Kenneth, Euan, and the rest of the senior Brodie scouts and fighters met with Iain the next morning. They settled around the large table in Iain's solar and waited for the laird to speak. He'd called them together with little notice. None of them knew why, but Calum was certain it meant there was trouble coming their way.

Was Domhnall coming back to finish what he'd started at Harlaw? A chill slid down Calum's back. A lot of good men died that day, and as far as he knew, their deaths accomplished nothing. Still, if Iain intended to take Brodie back into that fight, Calum wanted to be a part of it. None of them would be able to resist the chance to finish the job, and to put an end to the threat of war in the Highlands. But how? He still couldn't trust that he would see anything coming at him on his left side in time to protect himself.

"I have news," Iain began without preamble. "First the good news. Annie heard from her elder sister at Rose that Cameron Sutherland is doing better." He raised a hand as smiles broke out around the table. "But the problem he and Kenneth encountered is still with us and has gotten worse. We've heard of more roving bands of men spreading out from the area west of Harlaw. They've been robbing travelers of weapons, coin and other valuables, attacking crofts and stealing food, both grains and meat. Some of it livestock they can herd along with them. The attacks had diminished during the last few sennights, and it appeared that they'd moved on, bypassing us westward, or farther south if they're from Mar's army, headed home. 'Tis nay longer the case. Crofts were looted and burned on our border to the south with Clan Grant last night."

Euan sat up straighter. "What do ye need us to do?"

"Scouts will go out first and do what scouts do. Locate any bands moving into or through Brodie territory. Some may be simply passing through. Peacefully. But we ken some are no'. Ye have my permission and that of our allies to stray into their territory as needed to apprehend any fighters who have stolen property in their possession. If ye are attacked, ye will defend yerselves. Be certain any encounters in neighboring territory are gallowglass men or lowlanders, and no' our allies. We dinna need to start trouble with Grant or any other nearby clan."

"When do we leave?" Kenneth glanced around the table, checking on his men without another word and getting nods in response.

"Get yer gear together today. Some of ye will leave after dark, others in the morning, so as not to alert any watchers who may be in the area that we're on the move. Or that this keep has fewer defenders. We dinna ken if the clans along the firth are being watched. But better no' to take that chance. The trouble Kenneth and Cameron Sutherland encountered happened near the coast. Kenneth, organize yer scout parties and the timing of their departures. If ye encounter any large groups, ye will return or send word and wait for reinforcements. Is that clear?"

"Aye," Kenneth answered for the rest of the men.

"Very well."

At Iain's nod, the men stood and filed out of the solar, all except Kenneth who likely wanted to discuss tactics with Iain. Calum hung back with Euan. He wanted a word with Kenneth.

"I ken what ye intend to say," Euan said in low tones, his expression serious. "Ye have spent little time sparring. Are ye willing to risk yer life on yer ability to see a blade coming from yer left side?"

"I'm a Brodie scout. 'Tis my duty to go where the laird sends me," Calum answered vaguely. He knew what he wanted. To be his old self, at the forefront of a battle. Yet Euan had a valid point. Joining the fight might not be possible yet. And was certainly not wise. Still, there was an option he liked even less—for Kenneth to order him to remain behind in Brodie. Though if raiders got into Brodie…nay, he would not think about what they might do to the clan's women. To Ella. She had already suffered too much harm from men—even men who were supposed to protect her. The memory of the day the Munro laird allowed Thomas Ross to reclaim her still made Calum want to punish the Munro with his fists. She and Muireall had longed to return home, never expecting that Ella would be forced to go back to her husband. Calum could not let another man hurt her ever again.

He and the other scouts would find where the raiders camped, and Brodie warriors would deal with them there. His nerves jangled, making it hard for him to stand still. He took a breath, trying to calm the tension swirling in his gut. Euan would notice any anxiety and put it down to fear rather than eagerness.

He wouldn't be entirely wrong.

So much of everything he hoped to regain depended on him being part of this. Scouting and finding the trouble-makers. Yet he wished they showed up a fortnight or more from now, when he was in better command of his abilities. "If I canna fight, I can still scout."

Euan studied him, speculation in his gaze. "Ye may be right. Ye're the best of us at moving silently, and ye notice everything around ye. Ye always have."

"I still do," Calum insisted, frowning as the memory filled him of walking about the bailey with Ella, his eyes covered, while she pretended to be Janet. His every other sense had been filled with sounds, smells, tastes, and changes in temperature. Even the rise and fall and the texture of the ground beneath his boots. And her. He'd known she was Ella. He simply hadn't wanted to admit it to himself.

"Kenneth may have already thought of using ye that way."

"If he hasna, I intend to convince him."

Euan nodded, the beginnings of a grin lifting the

corners of his lips. "Saint Gertrude's anklebones, Calum, welcome back."

Calum did grin at that, but quickly wiped it away as the door to Iain's solar opened and Kenneth stepped out.

"I thought I might find ye…both…here," he said, glancing from Calum to Euan and back to Calum. "Ye are on scout duty. Aye, both of ye," he added as Calum's mouth opened to question him. "Ride and hide and report. Dinna engage. Euan, ye are good with weapons, and Calum is at a disadvantage for now. Keep him out of trouble. Calum, ye are better than any man at noticing things others miss, but if at any time ye find ye canna continue—"

"That willna happen," Calum assured him.

"Very well. Ye leave after dark. I expect ye both back alive and in one piece, aye?"

"Aye," they answered together.

Elated, Calum wanted to pump a fist in the air, and to shout that he was still a Brodie scout. Still one of the best. And now he had a chance to prove it. Somehow, he held it in.

Kenneth nodded and left them, likely on his way to tell his wife Catherine, and to ready his own pack and weapons.

"Good news, aye?" Euan said with a grin and clapped Calum on his shoulder. "'Tis too early in the day to cele-brate. I'll meet ye in the bailey at midday and we can spar."

"We can drink when we get back. Training is the only celebration I need right now. As long as ye dinna take my head from my shoulders."

"Or do anything else that would keep ye from leaving

this night, aye. I ken how important this is to ye. 'Tis important to me for ye to be ready, as well. Despite Kenneth's wishes, we may have to fight."

"No' if I can prevent it," Calum told him, determined to keep them out of trouble. For him to be fully accepted, they must succeed.

❧

"Have ye heard?"

Muireall's voice snapped Ella out of the daydream she'd been having as she folded dry bedding she'd helped pull from the lines before the latest rain shower blew through. In her musings, Calum had come to her and apologized. Begged her forgiveness. Sworn his undying love and devotion, then kissed her senseless. Almost. Muireall entering her chamber pulled her from her fantasy before it got any better, damn it.

"Heard what?" She dropped what she was doing and faced her friend.

Muireall took one look at her and grinned. "And what's been on yer mind, eh? Ye are blushing. Have ye talked to Calum about training ye yet like I suggested?"

"Naught to do with ye, and nay. I dinna ken if I can face him when he turns me down." She waved a hand in front of her face as if brushing aside that idea. "What news have ye brought me?"

Muireall crossed her arms, looking for a moment as if she'd continue to interrogate Ella, but she sobered. "The scouts are going out. Starting tonight, looking for bands of men who've been stealing from travelers, and looting and burning crofts. Gallowglass men, they think, left behind from the army Domhnall took to Harlaw."

"'Tis terrible news," Ella said, realizing what this meant. "There will be fighting."

"Aye, likely. Though scouts have been told to avoid it and report back if they find any large groups of men."

"How many men are going?"

"Dinna ye mean, is Calum going? Aye, he is. With Euan at least, who will keep him safe. They're first out. Tonight."

Ella dropped onto the bed, her knees weak. "He canna fight. Why would Iain send him?"

"Because he's needed. Ye ken he's one of the best scouts. They both ken he's vulnerable. Euan will protect him. They'll avoid trouble and come back here to report anything they find."

Ella thought back to her walk around the bailey with Calum while his eyes were still covered. She had done her best to convince him that with his other senses, he was still a Brodie scout. "It's what he's lived for," she told Muireall. "So why does the idea now make my heart race?"

"Because it is again real," Muireall told her. "No' just something he hopes for."

"What if he gets hurt—or killed?" She forced herself to her feet. "I should speak to him. Apologize. I canna let him go into danger feeling about me—about us—the way he does."

"'Tis after the midday meal. He and Euan will be on the practice ground. But Ella, he is preparing for his first mission since he was hurt. He may no' want to speak with ye. And to confront him where the other men can see and hear? I wouldna."

"I'll wait nearby 'til they're done."

"Where he can see ye? Ye'll distract him when he needs to focus on proving himself. And if he gets hurt there because he notices ye, and he canna go tonight, he'll blame ye, and ye will lose him forever."

Ella sank back down onto the bed. "What should I do? I have to see him before he leaves."

Muireall sank down beside her and picked up her hand, giving it a comforting squeeze. "Dinna fash. I have an idea. I'll help ye."

THE GREAT HALL was already filled with the low rumble of conversation when Calum arrived for an early supper with Euan. He'd thought to eat before the hall became crowded, but it seemed the word spread about the scouts going out to hunt raiders, and everyone gathered to learn more.

He and Euan would not leave for hours yet. Daylight faded earlier this time of year, but they must wait for full dark to escape detection. The later it got, the more eager Calum became.

Euan found him waiting at the entrance to the hall, watching it fill.

"Iain wants a word," he told him.

Calum froze. Was Iain about to tell him he was going to confine him to the keep? After Kenneth's vote of confidence, he'd never expected to get pulled from this mission, but why else would Iain summon them now save to give Euan time to find another partner tonight? With a heavy heart, Calum followed his friend to the laird's solar. Euan entered and stepped aside to let Calum enter. But then Euan pivoted behind him, out of the chamber and closed the door. Calum wheeled to the door, surprised. What was Euan up to? When he turned back around, he knew.

"Ye." Not Iain.

Ella stood up from her chair by the hearth, her hands twisting together in front of her waist.

So, another deception, and this time, Euan was in on it. Muireall, no doubt, asked him to do this. Was there no one he could trust?

"Dinna leave," Ella said softly. "I need to speak with ye before ye go out tonight."

"Aye? Do ye have information about these gallowglass men we're to find?"

Her eyes widened at the sarcasm in his tone. "Nay, of course no'."

"Then we've naught to discuss."

Her lips thinned in response to his curt comment. "Calum, I'm sorry. I have regretted my actions every moment since ye saw me in the healer's doorway. Even before then."

"As ye should."

She paled, making him regret being so abrupt with her. But Euan had led him into an ambush, so he didn't feel like he owed her kindness. Somehow, he'd survive it—and find a way to make Euan regret this.

"Can ye ever forgive me? I care about ye. Ye ken that. I wanted to help ye heal. Is that so terrible?"

She was persistent. He'd give her that. He couldn't let her get to him. Calum glanced around at the solid doorway behind him. "Euan brought me here. So I'm to understand that he and Muireall think I should forget yer lies and—"

"Nay. Aye. But nay. Ye must do as ye think best." She hesitated and swallowed, as if dreading his reaction. "But before ye risk yer life again, I wanted to tell ye how sorry I am. And that I miss the friendship we had before ye were hurt. How we seemed to be growing closer and happier all the time. I…I want that back."

For one wild moment, Calum did, too. Then he sobered. This was Ella's power. Not her beauty, though that didn't hurt. Her strength was in her kindness. Her regard for the feelings of others. Her determination to help, even when her help was not wanted. His pride wouldn't let him fall for it.

His pride. That was his weakness. What would it harm to give her a crumb of forgiveness? Doing nothing would be cruel, and that was not in his nature. If something happened and he didn't come back from this mission, he could give her that small comfort rather than leaving her convinced he didn't care for her. Or that he didn't want her, when clearly he had. He'd been relentless in his pursuit of her, despite her history. She was the one who deserved to be proud. Not shamed. Not treated the way he'd been treating her. She probably thought that now, after what she'd done, even though her motives had been good, he hated her. And he didn't. Mostly, he hated himself.

"Ye ask for something I dinna ken how to give. We canna go back. And perhaps we shouldna. But I can give ye this, in case I dinna return. In case ye find yerself standing over my cold, dead body."

She flinched at his words.

That slight movement told Calum more than anything else that she truly did care for him. That forgiving her was the right thing to do. For her, but for himself, as well. He found that he didn't have to force out the words. They came easily. "I forgive ye, Ella. I accept that ye meant well. I forgot that ye dinna have it in ye to do anything as cruel as what I accused ye of. I let my pain and my fear cloud my judgment and cause me to strike out at ye. I'm sorry, too."

Her beautiful eyes overflowed with tears. "Then perhaps we have a way forward, Calum. A way past all of this."

He shook his head. "I dinna ken how. I'm sorry, but I dinna. I forgive ye, but I willna forget that ye lied to me."

He turned and opened the door, but her soft cry made him pause and glance back at her.

"Come home to me, Calum," she said. "Dinna let yer pride get ye killed this night or any other."

He nodded and left the solar, carefully closing the door behind him. She would need some time to herself. He leaned against it, resting the back of his head on the thick, hard oak, taking deep breaths to calm his racing heart. He'd tried to help her, but with his final words, he'd hurt her again. And for what? His damned pride. But if he went back in there to apologize, he would only make things worse.

He had to do something—anything—else. Food would wait. First, he wanted to flatten his arms master and scouting partner for doing much the same as Ella had done. Lying to him, and setting him up for the encounter he'd just bungled with her. Euan owed him for this, but he changed his mind before he stepped away from the door.

Euan might owe him for this, but he was the one who'd failed Ella—and himself. Ella had given him a chance to make amends. The danger he was going into this night was only the excuse. If, nay, when he came back, they could have begun again from a better place than where they started when he walked into Iain's solar. He'd ruined that chance.

CHAPTER 7

Three long days passed while Ella paced and fretted. Muireall was only a little better, worried for her husband Euan, but confident that he could take care of himself in a fight. Knowing Calum's vision was not perfect, Ella couldn't share her certainty, but took some comfort knowing that Euan would guard his left side if it came to a fight.

The lack of news worried all of them. At last, Muireall tired of her long face and dragged her outside, to where the lasses held their archery target practice against the inside of the keep's outer curtain wall, something Muireall suggested several times, but Ella had refused to do in the year since she'd come to Brodie.

Ella was still reluctant, more interested in learning to heal than in injuring or killing. But she'd seen in July how it felt to have most of the fighting men away from the keep with Domhnall's army, and how the women, trained as archers, kept watch on the wall walk and made everyone feel safer. If she needed more convincing, one look at Annie's young lad and the idea of helping to keep the clan's bairns safe soothed her qualms.

Had they lost many men at Harlaw, and thank they saints they had not, those women would have been even more important defending the clan until the younger lads and lasses grew older, stronger, and more skilled. Now that Brodie was again without a number of their warriors, refreshing her observations from July, she decided it was time for her to step up. Iain sent out all of their scouts and a third of their fighting men. He remained in the keep, as did Annie. She drilled the women who'd already become skilled archers, while bringing up other lasses who wanted to join their more experienced sisters in defending the clan.

Ella wanted to learn to defend the keep, while hoping she never actually had to. So, she went with Muireall to a sheltered corner of the bailey where targets were set up, nervous but determined.

"Ye need a distraction, and this one is useful," Muireall said as she took Ella to a stack of bows of varying lengths and began having her try them for size and pull. "Ye'll train with the newer lasses," she added. "Ye canna place a value on learning to defend yerself."

"How long will it take me to learn to do this?" Each bow Muireall gave her seemed too large, and pulling it required more strength than she possessed. But Muireall was undeterred and when one bow proved to be too much, handed her another.

"That depends on ye. A day or two for the basics, but longer to practice and become an expert."

"That could take me—"

"Sennights, or months, aye, but consider this, if ye get good at archery, Calum might respect ye more, since archery and fighting are things he understands and values."

"That's a good point. Helping Mhairi has no' served me well with him."

"Give him time, Ella. Yerself, too. Ye will find a way. And ye will want to spend some time with Iain's lot as well."

"I've watched them a wee when I passed nearby. This is hard, but what they're doing looks harder. And more dangerous."

Muireall hesitated, then said, "After what ye have been through, learning to protect yerself will make ye feel stronger and more confident."

Ella nodded. She didn't like to think about their time at Ross, but Muireall was right.

At her nod, Muireall continued, "The biggest danger in training is getting bruised. But every lass should ken how to protect herself. 'Tis easier than trying to shoot someone with an arrow when they've already got their hands around yer throat."

"Ye have a point."

Muireall nodded as Ella found a bow she could pull, then handed her a fistful of arrows. "Let's do this first. Later, I can show ye some simple moves—"

"Aye, show me."

"But after, ye must promise me to also learn from Iain. Or Calum." She grinned, then sobered. "Either of them will teach ye more than I can. Especially Calum." Her grin came back.

Ella ignored what Muireall likely thought Calum could teach her. "If I agree to work with Iain, why no' go with me? Surely there is more ye wish to learn."

Muireall considered for a moment. "Ye have a point," she said, echoing Ella's earlier comment.

"I hope everyone is back soon," Ella said as Muireall chose a target for her to use and set her in place. "Even though we went through this in July, it seems strange to have so many of the men out of the keep at once."

"So many men out of the keep, or one particular one? I recall how ye worried over Calum while he was gone this summer."

Muireall helped Ella line up a shot, then she pulled and let it fly. She grimaced as it fell short of the target by several feet. "With good reason, as it turned out," she answered while picking up another arrow and nocking it. "I took yer advice. Did Euan tell ye before they left?"

"That he made certain ye had a chance to speak to Calum, aye. But he didna ken what happened, except that he thought Calum needed the time to get over whatever the two of ye said to each other. Does that mean it didna go well?"

Ella lowered her bow, suddenly unable to summon the strength to pull it. She was grateful to have a friend like Muireall. Someone she could talk to. Someone who knew first-hand what she'd been through at Ross. But with all of that, she wasn't sure she could repeat what she and Calum said to each other. She'd break down before she got very far.

"I see," Muireall said before Ella recovered enough to have a chance to answer. "Ye will tell me when ye are ready. When ye are able."

"I…he said he forgave me."

"Did he? The bastard."

"What?" Why would Muireall say that? Ella thought they all wanted him to forgive her. She certainly did.

Muireall planted her fists on her hips. "Ye had done naught that needed forgiveness." Then she shrugged. "I'm disappointed in him that he continues to think so."

"And so, naught has changed." Ella pursed her lips. Nothing had changed, and likely never would.

"Nay. I think something has."

"What do ye mean?"

Muireall patted her hand. "He bent enough to offer ye some ease before he left, in case he didna come back. His pride is a fearsome thing, but it showed a crack when he made the effort to comfort ye. And a cracked wall can be broken."

THE THING CALUM hated most about scout duty was spending nights in the cold and often wet without a fire to warm him. He and Euan couldn't risk one being seen, and they were not far enough into a rocky area to be able to hide one behind boulders. Daytime was no better. Smoke could be seen for miles. So they wore layers of clothing and wrapped themselves in warm woolen plaids, with an outer layer of oiled wool to keep them as dry as possible. It sufficed for a night or two. Longer than that and they'd normally seek better shelter, but their quarry might well be doing the same thing, increasing his and Euan's chances of being discovered before they had a chance to find the raiders.

He spent their rest time while Euan was on watch trying to sleep and obsessing about Ella, rethinking everything that had happened between them from the moment he first saw her as a captive in the Ross camp with Muireall and the third Munro lass, Tira, who'd stayed with her Ross husband. He recalled all Ella had said and done as herself and as Janet while he recuperated. All the times she'd encouraged him, and kept him from wrecking his recovery. He'd thought he knew her before he was injured, but his fears and anger affected his perspective. The more he mulled it over, the more he saw her intentions for what they had been—good for him. He'd been right to forgive her, even if he'd done so reluctantly at the time. Could he accept that and move forward toward her? With her?

By the third night, Calum came to the conclusion that he had no answers. Life was a gamble. He and Euan were accustomed to this work. Proud of it, truth be told. And damned good at it. And they were lucky. Someday that luck might run out, but they did all they could to hold off that day's arrival by being smart. And careful. And well trained. Their mounts, too, were trained to silence when it was needed, their tack oiled and checked constantly against rattles and clinks. Hand signals sufficed when the sound of a voice might give them away to an enemy.

There was just enough starlight filtering through gaps in the tree canopy for Calum to use one now and know Euan would see it. He'd heard something. A whisper of sound. Perhaps an owl or a wildcat. Or a man. His signal stopped Euan and they waited, still and silent as the night. The wind had died with the sunset, and the normal forest sounds like the calls and fluttering wings of birds, and the wind sighing through pine branches, had quieted, too.

He heard it again. The suggestion of a sound. Perhaps something in the distance, but it didn't pay to make assumptions. It might come from something behind the next tree. Or above them in the canopy. Without turning his head, he used his eyes to scan as much around them as he could. But his left-side night vision was no better than his vision during the day. His hearing would have to tell him where and what they faced.

Or would it? His nostrils flared. A sudden light breeze carried a scent. Upwind was to his right. He concentrated, soaking in anything his senses told him came from that direction. Euan was close enough to see him cant his head that way, so he counted on Euan to focus elsewhere, covering the other approaches an enemy might use to surprise them. They could well be upwind of trouble, themselves.

They waited.

A soft cough nearly startled Calum into a reaction. Instead, a satisfied smile curled his lips. Got ye. Now, was it one man or many? A lone guard outpost for a larger group farther in that direction? Or one man acting alone or separated from his fellows?

The night stayed quiet until an owl's hoot broke the stillness.

"Shite."

That grumbled oath had to have come from the man he heard cough.

Silence fell again. Calum waited. If there were two or more, someone else would speak and he would hear the difference in the voice. The night remained silent.

The owl hooted again.

Calum's hackles rose. Was that truly an owl, or a signal? Had he and Euan been spotted? He fought the urge to dismount or ride away, and continued to wait, tense now, his senses open to any new sounds, new movement. Anything that would give away an ambush.

He heard nothing save normal night sounds. Those would have stopped if any predator, two-legged or four, came near.

After a lengthy wait, he nodded to Euan and slipped silently off his patient horse and paused, listening for any change in the night. Hearing nothing, he signed his intentions to Euan, then he moved like the soft breeze from tree to tree, brush to bramble, careful of his footing on the loamy forest floor. Pine needles made a soft, spongy carpet. But one misstep and a twig's snap would alert his quarry. Calum did not make missteps. The closer he got, the more of the man's sweaty stench wafted to him on the night breeze. He paused again and heard deep, regular breathing. His quarry was nearby and asleep or close to it. The breath sounds were loud enough for Calum to locate him in the dark, mere feet away, seated on the ground, leaning against a tree. Alone, and now nodding off. A sentry. A poor one. Where were the rest? And were they as lax in their duty as this man?

Calum could slit his throat before he took his next breath. He would never cry out.

But he and Euan weren't here for that. Calum was charged with finding the rest of the group, determining if they were some of the troublemakers, then reporting their location back to Iain. He eased away, keeping his gaze focused for any sign of movement from the dozing man or anything else near him. If the sentry kept his back to the direction he knew to be safe, then it made sense that his fellow raiders, if that was who they were, camped in that same direction.

Calum slipped past the sentry, keeping silent and, nerves tingling, even more careful. He could be approaching another sentry or the main camp filled with any number of men. He crept forward again, using the forest as cover, pausing often to listen to the night sounds. Before long, the scent of a campfire and of roasting meat reached him. A glimmer of light flickered through gaps between the trees, and a few paces farther, the murmur of low voices rewarded him.

He dared not approach too closely. There must be more sentries in these woods, and the same firelight that revealed their base could also betray him. He paused at his first view of the camp. In a small clearing, a dozen men sat around a low fire where a sheep roasted atop stones. Behind them, against the background trees, another one bleated, destined, he supposed, to be tomorrow's dinner. Calum estimated a band of at least sixteen men, accounting for other sentries he expected were arrayed around their base, perhaps more. The campfire alone told him there were enough of them that they were not concerned about being seen. This group was large enough to do damage to crofts and small villages. And to make quick work of him and Euan. Another owl called, but the men didn't react. So it hadn't been a signal.

He turned around and put his back against a broad trunk so his vision would readjust to the forest's darkness. There, he waited and listened until he was certain he heard Irish accents and even Irish Gaelic. A few of the men began boasting about what they'd gotten from the last croft they'd raided. Including what they'd done to a woman there. His fists clenched, wanting to kill them all for that.

Then he heard footsteps approaching. One of the men had left the campfire, perhaps to relieve himself, or to replace the sleeping guard Calum found. But judging by the direction of the man's tread, he would pass within inches of where Calum waited. Too close. Even if he didn't see Calum in the deeper darkness, he might sense his presence.

There wasn't much time to create a distraction before he'd be discovered. He pulled his slingshot from inside his leine and a few pebbles from the bag he always carried tied at his waist when he left Brodie. Slinging one after the other, he launched them off to one side of the camp, careful to ensure they weren't visible in the firelight. He aimed at tree trunks and, where he could tell some had collected, bounced a few into dry leaves. Both of those would make as much noise as he dared to create. It would take only one small stone falling into view for them to know the noise they heard wasn't made by a large number of men, and so didn't herald an attack. And they'd come looking for him.

He couldn't move closer either, so he wasn't tempted to hit any of the men unless he had to silence the one headed his way in order to protect himself. He wouldn't use the slingshot for that.

But the man headed his way stopped and muttered, "What—", then turned back toward the fire and his compatriots. "I heard something."

Calum sent a few more rocks into the trees.

The man pointed off to his right as he reached the fire. "That way," he shouted, bent and grabbed his sword. "Who are ye, ye bastards? Show yerselves!"

Calum slung more stones toward the opposite side of the camp and heard another man warn, "We're being surrounded." As Calum moved quickly from shadow to shadow away from the commotion he'd caused, he heard the men milling around, pulling weapons out of scabbard's and heading in different directions, an anthill thoroughly stirred and furiously disturbed.

He kept several trees between him and the guard he'd found earlier. The man was on his feet now, peering through the dark back toward the camp as the noise there carried into the forest, masking Calum's careful footfalls.

Calum didn't wait to see if he would abandon his post and go to join his fellows.

Back with Euan a few minutes later he didn't need silence, but he kept his voice low. "Ye hear that? We need to go, now." He swung up onto his horse and pulled the reins around to head quietly back the way they'd come.

"Did ye cause that uproar?" Euan snorted. "Of course ye did. Dammit, man, I was about to decide I was going to have to come save ye."

"I wouldha stopped ye before ye got into the midst of the trouble," Calum assured him. Once they were far enough from the raiders to be certain they hadn't been pursued, he nodded to Euan. "Let's ride! We've something to report."

BACK AT BRODIE soon after sunrise, they turned their mounts over to the stable lads and went straight to Iain.

"There were enough men in that camp to have caused most or all of the trouble the other clans are reporting. I counted a dozen at their fire, plus one confirmed sentry. I would expect at least three more arrayed around the camp, maybe more," Calum said. He explained how he'd made them think they were surrounded and dispersed them to avoid being found by one of them headed his way. "And I heard Irish voices and boasts about what they'd done. After I disturbed them and they didn't find anyone, chances are they think those woods are haunted, and they've moved on."

"We took a circuitous route back in case we were noticed and followed," Euan added. "We werena."

"Good. Nay sense in leading them here. Kenneth returned late yesterday without encountering any strangers." Iain paused, then straightened, some decision made. "Euan, get together with him. Ye ken the way. Take enough men with ye to round up that entire band, assuming they're no' scattered all over the countryside." He grimaced, then grinned at Calum. "We'll gift any who survive to the Marshall with my blessings."

"Even if they moved from where we found them during the night, a group that large will leave a trail," Euan said. "We'll find them again."

Iain nodded. "First, go speak to yer wife. She'll have my hide if I send ye out again without a chance to see ye. Dinna take too long."

Euan grinned. "I'll be as quick as she'll let me," he quipped and left them.

Calum waited for Iain to dismiss him as well, but the laird clearly had something else on his mind.

"Ye proved yer skill and yer worth to Brodie yet again, Calum. Because of that, I dinna want to risk ye in a fight. No' until ye are certain ye can defend yerself. Ye have earned a rest. Yer role in this willna be overlooked."

He started to object to being left behind, but kept his complaint behind his teeth. Iain was right. He wasn't ready to survive in the midst of an all-out fight. He appreciated Iain's praise and accepted his laird's resolve to keep him safe until he was able to protect himself and the men around him, rather than to be a burden. "Thank ye, laird."

Iain nodded. Calum took that as dismissal and headed out into the great hall. Several of the men who'd just come off night duty on the wall walk had taken seats near the hearth. He joined them. Finally, warm and dry and with an ale in him, he answered their questions about his and Euan's scouting mission until he noticed the sky visible through a high window beginning to brighten.

"The rest of the clan will be here soon to break their fasts," he said, indicating the window where he'd noticed the early morning glow. "I'm going to turn in." Iain's praise and these men's easy acceptance of his presence had warmed him, but he expected he'd have much more to do later today. He must get some rest.

"Aye, ye'll never get away if ye dinna go now," one of the men told him. "We'll be right behind ye."

CALUM HEARD someone coming up the stairs after he reached the upper hallway. Not one of the men. The steps were too light. A lass, or one of the younger lads. He waited until they reached the top. His awareness of what was around him was heightened while he waited for whomever followed him. The lads he'd been drinking with hadn't moved when he did, so this was someone else. The closer the steps came the more certain he knew who was coming up. In moments, her scent convinced him.

Ella. As she stepped up into the hallway, Calum reached out and gently grasped her arm. She stifled a shriek of surprise, then relaxed when she saw him.

"Of course ye kenned I was coming," she said. "Ye sensed me, did ye?"

He released her arm, confident she wouldn't run away. "I heard ye. Smelled ye, too, on the last few steps. I ken the way ye move. Yer gait. Yer scent." He let his gaze bore into her, and was gratified to see color rise from her chest to her face. It was a reminder of their walk in the bailey, and of her attempt to disguise herself as Janet. Of course, she would react as if embarrassed.

But rather than quail under his scrutiny, she stared back and let the corner of her lips lift. "I canna get away with anything around ye," she quipped.

He grinned, his attention on her full lips. Suddenly, the urge to taste them consumed him. He fought it down. "So ye havena learned yer lesson?" He thought his question would fall flat, since clearly they were talking about Janet, not her.

But she took the bait. "If that lesson has to do with ye, probably no'," she told him, "though I'm honestly no' sure which lesson ye refer to."

This was no place for a private conversation. Or anything else. He took her hand, and when she didn't object, he walked with her down the hall away from the stairs, so their voices wouldn't carry to the men still seated by the hearth fire. "I've spent three cold, dark nights thinking about what ye said before I left," he told her when they stopped outside his chamber. His pulse picked up. Would her response be very bad, or very good? Would they end up inside his door?

"And?" She kept her voice steady as she asked the question, but judging by the pulse beating in the smooth column of her throat, her heart must be thundering in her chest.

Calum stopped and turned to face her. "I still care about ye. Still want ye." He held up his free hand. "Though I shouldna. I still dinna ken what to do about ye. Whether I can trust ye."

Ella pulled her fingers from his, irritation evident in the crease between her brows. "I've admitted my mistake. Apologized. Ye said ye forgave me. Have I no' earned even a small measure of trust?"

Had she? How would he know if he could trust her, and if she truly wanted him? If she wanted them to become the most important people in each other's lives, able to live together and love each other, and to build a family and a future together, she would have to tell him. And show him.

Though he knew it shouldn't, the glint in her narrowed eyes hurt. He'd made her angry, when what he wanted was for her to talk to him, to explain why he was so important to her that she would do what she'd done. "Trust takes time to build. To be earned."

He wasn't saying no to her question. At worst he thought she would argue. At best, she might agree to give them some more time together. And admit how deeply she cared for him. How could he convince her?

He gave in to his urge, pulled her in, and kissed her.

Ella froze for a moment, clearly surprised. He'd never dared such intimacy with her before. A light touch on her shoulder, or an arm around her waist if she needed support, less like the time he scooped Janet up against his chest to prevent her falling, but enough to show his care and concern. That was all. He'd never even kissed her hand or her cheek. Now, she slipped one hand up his chest and cradled the back of his neck, her fingers tangling in his hair. Her other arm wrapped around his waist and held onto him as firmly as he restrained her.

He'd been right to do this. Kissing her seemed the most natural, most necessary thing in the world. Why had he waited so long? Her scent filled him, her taste teased his tongue, so he traced the seam of her mouth, all the while feeling his need for her build. If he didn't stop soon, he wouldn't be able to.

She was a tempest in his arms, kissing him back as fervently as he kissed her. She was no untried virgin. But the way she trembled in his arms, he suspected her passion, the heat she was showing him, was new to her. He had to stop this before they both lost control. As much as he wanted to pull her into his chamber and kick the door closed, he couldn't do it. He would not go from one kiss— their first kiss—to ravaging her minutes later. He was a better man than that, and she deserved better from him than to treat her like a common harlot.

When he broke the kiss, she sucked in some badly needed air, and desire darkened her gaze. "So, there is a future for us," she said softly, gratefully.

He stiffened and let her go, suddenly reluctant to cede victory in this skirmish to her. He'd just told her that trust took time to earn. Then he'd kissed her. This was his fault. "Maybe."

She had passion. That kiss proved it better than any

other indication she'd shown him. She'd kissed him back with no reserve. She wanted him as much as he wanted her. And that was very good news.

"Calum, ye just kissed me like yer wound never happened. Like we are still as dear to each other as before, and ye want us to be even closer."

He couldn't tell her how much that kiss meant to him. It would give away too much. "Or I kissed ye like I just had my biggest success since I was injured, and wanted to enjoy it. To be rewarded for it. Ye followed me for a reason. That wasna it?"

"Rewarded!" She opened her mouth to say more, and then closed it and shook her head.

Calum tensed, certain he wouldn't like whatever was coming, but he needed to deflect her from thinking their kiss proved something more than he'd meant for it to. He'd kissed her on impulse. Because he wanted to. That was all.

"I heard what ye told the men downstairs. Ye didna brag. Ye simply told them what happened and accepted their praise with grace. I was proud of ye. I wanted to tell ye that."

His muscles loosened, and he lifted a hand to trace a finger along her cheek, but thought better of touching her. Despite her kind words, she still looked furious. "Thank ye, then. For that," he added.

"What are ye trying to do here?"

Her challenging tone sparked his own irritation and he narrowed his eyes at her. "Perhaps I needed to find out who would kiss me back. Who ye are today? Ella lied to me, but Janet was my friend. Ella ignored my pursuit of her for months, but Janet served me faithfully. Ella is delicate and shy, but Janet is not afraid to touch me. So, which one of you kissed me back?"

Her jaw flexed, and her brow drew down. "Both of us, Calum. Both of us have touched ye." Her gaze dropped below his waist, and then lifted to his lips. "Both of us kissed ye. I hope ye enjoyed it, for it will never happen again."

Without another word, Ella turned from him. She didn't run. She walked, back stiff, insult radiating from her, head held high, and her hands clenched into fists.

For one wild moment, he felt those hands on his body, washing him, turning him, while she murmured to him that all would be well. Memory? Or imagination? Either made him profoundly uncomfortable in a way that her touch with a different purpose, a more pleasurable purpose, would not. But the flash of feeling confirmed her assertion that she had indeed touched him while he lay unconscious. Intimately. His objection to her care had come too late to prevent it. And she'd still cared about him enough to lie to him. Enough to kiss him just now with such abandon that he'd been the one to call a halt. To pull back before they both melted from the heat and succumbed to the pull toward something they weren't ready for. Sanity prevailed—barely.

He'd angered her. That didn't bother him, though it should. He preferred her anger to the sadness that she had thrown like a dark cloak around her since they'd first argued. Since he'd first pushed her away.

She'd stood her ground when he challenged her in the

herbal. Even when the healer spoke up to defend her, she hadn't wilted or turned to the older woman for help. Her gaze stayed on him, direct and with an element of fury he'd never seen before from the sweet-natured Ella—until, again, now. He respected that, and recognize that, indeed, the traits he associated with Janet were, and always had been, a part of Ella. A part she'd had no reason to expose until he rejected her.

Still, he dared not make anything easy for her. His pride still stung from her deception. And she had put him off for months, claiming friendship, but not allowing what was between them to grow, to go any further toward a close— and physical—relationship. He hadn't blamed her, not after what she'd been through at Ross, and what she'd had to do to gain her freedom from Thomas Ross, starving herself.

What kind of woman went to such an extreme? A woman with more steel in her backbone than most, despite her soft and lovely exterior, that's who. He couldn't believe it had taken him this long to see how strong she was.

When she disappeared down the stairs, he entered his chamber and dropped onto his bed with a heavy sigh. Her anger satisfied something in him that he did not want to name. His pride? He'd already admitted to himself that his pride was a weakness. He clasped his hands between his knees, his gaze on the floorboards between his booted feet.

What did he think he was doing, letting that pride get between Ella and him?

He stood, torn between giving them both time to cool off while he got some sleep, and going after her. He glanced around with distaste at the bed he'd spent so many weeks in, blind, angry, and fearful. He shuddered at the idea of sleeping here any longer. The memories of lying there chilled him.

But dare he chase Ella? He'd be giving in to her. Before he and Euan went scouting, he'd told her he accepted her apology and forgave her. He'd meant it as absolution in case he didn't come back, so that she didn't carry the burden of what went wrong between them for the rest of her life. Now that he was back, was his forgiveness still real?

Had he lied to her in the same way she lied to him? For good reason or out of kindness? Was what he'd done any better than what she'd tried to do for him?

No, it wasn't.

So why wasn't he halfway down the stairs by now, calling her name?

His damned pride. He couldn't do it. Not now, not so publicly. And perhaps never, given the wall he just caused her to erect between them.

He collapsed back down onto the mattress and sank his head into his hands, tangling his fingers into his hair. He wasn't just insufferably proud. Where Ella was concerned, he was a coward.

CHAPTER 8

Head held high, Ella turned her back on Calum and walked away. She already regretted following him. But she did not regret that kiss. She'd waited for months for him to take her in his arms and kiss her. Her near-fall in the bailey didn't count. He'd saved her, but that had been his only intention. He'd made no move to take advantage of their closeness. And perhaps she should take comfort in that. At the time, he'd thought she was Janet, and he'd taken care of her as he would any lass who needed help.

Tonight, he had indeed taken advantage of her. Of Ella. It was as much her fault as his, but she didn't regret it. Instead, her body still hummed with longing while burning with irritation and insult at how he still berated her. How he'd compared her behavior and Janet's.

Her heart had lifted to see him back safe. But they couldn't go on like this. She couldn't live in the same keep and avoid the man who'd once been her friend. They

125

would have to come to some resolution. A truce. Some sort of comfortable indifference at least.

She thought back to the conversation she'd overheard as Calum matter-of-factly described how he found the raiders' camp. His even-toned recounting impressed her. He didn't brag. With the beating his pride had taken lately, she wouldn't have blamed him if he had.

She'd known when she did it that the urge to follow him would be foolish, a mistake, a risk she shouldn't take. But Muireall's advice had still been loud in her head. *Go after what ye want.*

So she gave in. She wanted to see him. To congratulate him, hoping perhaps he'd be in a more receptive mood after the success of his mission and his opportunity to tell other Brodie warriors about it.

Receptive didn't begin to describe it. That kiss! His lips were warm and firm as they pressed against hers, the hint of his breath ripe with the scent of ale and him. Her heart threatened to beat out of her chest as her blood heated under his caress. Her lips had parted a little as she sighed with contentment. In answer, his began to move lightly over hers, pressing, lighting fires in her body that she'd never felt before. When the tip of his tongue traced the seam of her lips, she shifted closer, putting their bodies more tightly together, reveling in the heat and solid strength of his chest under her hands. Since the day he'd held Janet, she'd missed being in his arms. She'd feared it might never happen again. Smiles and longing glances hardly counted. But this! He was a furnace against her body, stoking the unfamiliar fire in her blood. She'd missed him so much, she never wanted that kiss or that embrace to end.

Her former betrothed, Dermott, had never inspired such longing in her. And when her husband tried to hold her this way, she felt trapped, a prisoner. But her surrender into Calum's embrace was what desire and love were supposed to feel like. She mourned the time wasted with the wrong man. And mourned that the fire the kiss ignited had gone wrong, like everything seemed to do between them, turning to accusations, irritation, and even anger.

His frown made a lie of what she thought she'd seen in his eyes and felt in his kiss. Her words had been a mistake. She just didn't know how bad until it was too late.

After a few minutes of trading barbs, she'd been determined to beat him at this game. But tears threatened. She forced herself to hold them inside, unwilling to give him the satisfaction of seeing how easily he affected her. Angered her. Hurt her. She had to get away from him. She'd cede this skirmish to him for now, certain he believed she owed him a victory. But she sensed that when he kissed her, she'd won, too, even if hers was a pyrrhic victory.

What was it about this man that he thrilled her one moment and infuriated her the next?

She realized he was doing to her what she had done to him since they met. Since she and Thomas Ross divorced. Since Calum saw a clear field to try to win her over. Pulling her to him, then pushing her away. Still wrestling with what to do about her. With her. Just as she had done to him.

Did he realize what he was doing? She couldn't be certain, but she suspected he knew exactly the game he played. It was a bit of payback, then. She could accept that, but not if it went on for very long.

❧

LATER THAT SAME DAY, word spread that Georgie and some of the other lads were missing from the keep. Calum knew the missing lads from weapons training, and he recognized Kyle in the stable where he went to saddle his horse before riding out to search for them, as one of their group.

"Come with me," he said, intending to have this conversation in Iain's presence. At the lad's panicked look, he told him, "Ye are no' in trouble, but yer friends may be. Do ye ken where they went?"

"Nay. No' exactly."

"Let's talk about what ye do ken." Calum took him to Iain, knowing Iain would tease out anything the lad knew that Calum might miss.

"Why didna ye go with them?" Iain's question made color rise in the lad's face. "Tell us what happened, lad."

"I didna feel well. Gregor thought I'd slow them down, so he told me to stay behind."

"And ye didna like that, did ye?"

"Nay, laird. I wanted to help, too, but I'm no' as fast as the rest of them. Nor as good with a bow. No' yet. But I will be." His chin jutted out, making him look stubborn and determined enough to reach his goal.

"Good lad," Calum said. "Ye will grow, and with practice, ye will get better. Maybe even better than Gregor, aye?"

Kyle grinned. "I would like that."

"I'll wager ye would," Iain said, drawing their attention back to him. "Did they say where they were going to go to hunt? And for what?"

"No' exactly. Into the woods. Coneys mostly. Birds. Whatever Cook always wanted hunters to bring back."

Iain nodded and Calum gave the lad a reassuring smile. Then, Calum and Iain exchanged a glance, both aware the Cook often wanted wild pig or boar. If the lads tried to take one of those, Calum might find their broken, bloodied bodies. There were a lot of woods surrounding the Brodie keep on three sides. With boars and raiders loose in them, too, the lads might find more trouble than they could handle.

"When ye leave the keep to go exploring, where do ye go?" Calum hoped Kyle knew enough to make possible finding the lads quickly. Or at least to narrow where he must search.

"South, toward the old stones," the lad said. "The glen is level for a long way in that direction and the burn attracts lots of animals. 'Tis easier to walk farther. We heard the stones are haunted. Did ye ken that?"

Calum nodded. "So 'tis said. But I have never seen a ghost there."

"Nor a Sith?"

"Nary a one." The more he kept Kyle talking, the more he might recall something that would help his friends.

The lad looked disappointed. "We havena, either."

"But the Sith are clever at hiding. Ye may yet find one."

"Dinna encourage this," Iain admonished. "So ye think they might have gone that way. South, rather than along the coast."

"Aye, probably."

Calum had what he wanted, and the lad didn't seem sure of anything more. "I was nearly ready to ride out to search when I found Kyle here in the stable. I'll take some others with me. We'll find the lads and bring them home safe." Calum stood, so Kyle did, too.

"Ye are the best we have," Iain said. "Be safe. But find them. And thank ye, Kyle."

In the great hall, he found Ella, Muireall, and two of their best female archers, ones Calum knew had also been trained by Iain to protect themselves and others with blades. They were dressed for riding. "We ken ye'll be going out. We're going with ye," Muireall said. "My brother is out there. And Euan isna here to watch yer back, so we will."

"It takes four lasses to do what yer husband does? He'll be pleased to hear of that."

"And a few of yer warriors, too," Ella added. "They're waiting in the bailey."

"So ye were planning to go even before ye found I would join ye."

Muireall averted her gaze, but only for a moment, then met his, and gave him a curt nod.

"I should come, too," Kyle said.

Calum gripped his shoulder. "Nay, lad. Ye have done yer part. Ye may have saved yer friends a great deal of trouble.

Now that we ken where to look, we'll find them. Ye have much to do here to prepare for when we return the horses to the stable."

Annie joined them. "I just talked Iain out of coming with ye. His place is here. As is mine," she added with a glance down at her rounding belly. "I ken Calum will find the lads. The rest of ye, keep him safe, aye?"

Calum appreciated their confidence in him, but not that they all thought he needed a phalanx of lasses to guard him. And the few men outside, as well, he supposed.

"We'll keep the lads safe, too," Ella answered for them all.

Calum had heard enough. "Let's go."

ELLA DIDN'T KNOW whether to be excited or nervous. They were going on a mission usually reserved for men, but with Muireall's brother among the missing and her friend's expertise with a bow, it made sense for her to accompany them. Muireall had included the other women, and thankfully, with Annie's implicit approval, Calum could not object. Nor, it seemed, had Iain.

She hoped they didn't run into any raiders. Calum would not be impressed by her own skill with a bow. But seeing her armed and ready for the kind of trouble he understood should make him think differently about her.

They left the keep and walked out into the bailey, past the four waiting men. In the stables, the lads had readied their mounts and tied their bows and arrows to their tack.

She noted dirks in scabbards alongside the saddles and suddenly wished she'd gotten the training with Iain that Muireall recommended. If they made it back safely from this, she vowed she would. Or perhaps she would even gather her courage and ask Calum.

Calum turned to Muireall when he saw the preparations already made. "Ye lot were going out, no matter who else went?"

"My brother is out there. Of course we were going with them," she said, indicating the men who'd waited for them. "We are going. Now with ye, as well." Her stern expression left no room for argument.

Calum shook his head. "Daft lasses. I ken I'm wasting my breath, but do ye have any idea what might happen to ye if ye are caught by raiders?"

"We'll fight. And we have ye big, strong men to help protect those of us not as skilled as some in protecting ourselves." Muireall's gaze shifted to Ella.

Ella narrowed her eyes at her friend. Muireall was reminding her about her failure to ask Calum to train her.

"Ye should stay here," Calum said, turning to Ella.

"I'm going." She gave him her strongest, most determined stare. Inside, she wasn't so sure, but her knees were not quaking, and she would not let him make her feel weak. She had her bow, and if necessary, she'd use the blade. "If any of the lads are hurt, maybe I can help them."

Calum frowned.

Of course, he must be thinking about how she'd helped him. Ella turned aside to hide her disappointment in checking her mount's tack and heard him move away.

"I remember when Annie and Euan taught us to ride," Muireall said to Ella over her mount's back. "Would ye have guessed we'd be glad of the skill we now have, to be able to do something like this."

Ella glanced toward Calum, but he was leading his horse out of the stable, ready to go. Good. He'd accepted their presence. As they mounted up, Ella smiled. Muireall's reminder was just the distraction she needed. She'd learned, and now was an excellent rider. She was learning archery, and was getting better at it, though not yet as good as Muireall. She could do what she needed. "I remember not being eager to get on these great beasts, but ye were happy to do anything that included spending time with Euan. And he with ye. I recall that he was afraid yer horse would run away with ye, so he made himself yer teacher. I'll bet that was just the start of things he taught ye."

Muireall snorted, taking her meaning, then gestured to their weapons. "Or that we'd ken how to use these." With a shrug, her gaze followed Calum as joined the men waiting outside. "Ye should have taken my advice and asked him about training ye. But perhaps searching for the lads will serve. We'll all work together to find the lads, but I'll wager of all the lasses in our group, his attention will be on ye. Ye will spend time with him while he shows ye what he is best at. Ye wanted a way to bolster his pride. Now ye have it."

"Aye, he'll be watching me. To make sure I dinna do something he doesna like," Ella said and mounted up. "I appreciate what ye are trying to do," she told Muireall, "but just because it worked for Euan and ye doesna mean it will work for me with Calum."

"We will ken soon enough." Muireall mounted and gestured toward the stable door. "After ye."

They rode out of the stable, and the men formed up around them.

Calum, at the fore, turned his horse to face them. "Chances are the lads didna plan to go far on foot," he said, "so likely didna bring enough water skins or plaids to use if they were delayed until dark—or later. We'll search nearby first and find their tracks. Keep an eye out for other riders. They may mean trouble. Let's go."

As they passed through Brodie's gateway, Muireall's face creased with worry. Ella noticed and told her, "Georgie is a good lad and wiser than his years. He'll keep them all safe."

They passed the standing stones after a mile or so, without finding any sign the lads had been there. Surely they would not have been able to resist stopping to find the forest spirits spoken of in the tales the lads had heard. Could Kyle have been wrong? If the lads followed the coast, they were now miles from where the searchers were looking for them.

After riding several miles into a heavily forested glen and finding nothing, Calum sent two of their group off at angles to try a different direction. But soon thereafter, he spotted signs the lads came this way.

"Look there, and there," he said and pointed out the signs he'd seen to one of the men and to Ella, who'd ridden up even with him when he stopped. Black blood and tufts of rabbit fur littered the ground, confirming they were going the right way.

"We're a long walk from the keep to bring back whatever they find. I dinna think the lads would have planned on doing this," Muireall said. "What are they thinking, coming this far?"

"This deep in the wood, they're probably lost," Calum said. He sent one of the remaining men back to have the ones who split off from the group rejoin them. "I never thought the lads would go so far, either," he admitted. "Set up a perimeter, make camp," he ordered. "I'll scout farther. They may be close."

As their remaining male escort and the other two female archers moved to do as Calum ordered, Muireall objected. "I should go with ye."

"Nay, ye should stay here. The lads might see the fire and come in on their own. And ye lot can defend yourselves if anyone else shows up. Ella, ye'll come with me."

Ella exchanged a glance with Muireall, who gave her a wide-eyed look that Ella interpreted to mean, *this is your chance*. Was this wise? She wasn't a fighter. If they ran into trouble—

"We'll no' be going far," Calum said, breaking into her thoughts as if sensing she needed reassurance.

"Go with him," Muireall told her. "Find my brother."

Put that way, Ella couldn't refuse. "We will," she assured her friend, then nodded to Calum. "Let's go."

As THEY HEADED FARTHER into the woods, Calum wondered if he had lost his mind. Ella wasn't a fighter, and in these trees, an archer's skills were practically useless. But he wanted to keep her close. To protect her. His senses were alive with the sights and scents around him, the feel of the breeze, the glow from the lowering sun, all heightened by her nearness. Something about being with Ella away from the keep made everything seem brighter and better. Sweeter.

He glanced aside at her. She looked composed. Not at all like a lass on a mission to save a numpty bunch of lads who should not be out of the keep at all, much less this far from it and with night coming on. He appreciated their impulse to help put food on the clan's tables while many of the men were away chasing raiders, but to go on their own, with no adults? And let themselves get lost in deep woods at sunset? He shook his head. Surely he'd been wiser than that when he was their age. He'd had to keep Euan out of trouble, after all.

He was glad Ella was here. If the lads were lost and confused, Ella's calm sweetness would help soothe them. Worse, if any were hurt, she might make the difference between life and death for them.

"Should we call out for them?"

Her quietly voiced question told Calum she was aware of the possibility of raiders in the area.

"No' yet," he told her. "I still see signs they came this way. Look there." He pointed to broken branches on a sapling tree and beyond that, several broken twigs on a low growing bush. "One of them has the sense to try to mark their trail, to keep from going in circles."

"Why no' simply backtrack, then?"

"I've only seen them marking a trail since we stopped to make camp for the night. Either they're tracking something, or near the camp, one of them realized they were well and truly lost." Calum gestured upward. "Those leaves block the angle of the sun and scatter the light, as do the clouds. They didna have enough light to help them." He frowned. "And it's getting darker under here. We willna be able to track them much farther until morning."

Ella lifted a hand to her heart. "Muireall will be so worried. We've got to find them soon."

Autumn chill was in the air. The night would be cold and damp. "Aye, we need to." He held up a hand. "Wait, I hear something."

They drew up and sat, silent. Listening. After a few moments, Ella nodded. She'd heard it, too. Something crashing through the underbrush. A deer? Or worse, a boar? Or if they were lucky, the lads.

Calum moved to intercept whatever was making the noise. Ella followed.

It was a lad.

"Gordy! Ye are safe," Calum told him as he dismounted and approached the lad, who clung to a sapling's low branch and stared as if he was seeing things.

"Ye found me." He looked ready to collapse, or to burst in to tears, but he stayed upright and stoic.

"We did. Where are the rest of yer friends?"

"They went on, after a deer. I couldna keep up." He pointed to blood on the torn leg of his trews. "I fell into brambles and got cut on a broken branch."

"Let me take a look," Ella said, dismounting and grabbing her water skin. She made the lad sit down, rinsed his wounds, and inspected his leg for any debris in the wounds and scratches. "'Tisna too bad, but we need to get ye back to Mhairi." She ripped a length of cloth from his pants leg and bound it around and over the deepest wound. "That should stop the bleeding for now." She handed him the water skin. "Drink, Gordy. Ye'll feel better."

"The rest of the lads are in a ravine," he said after he satisfied his thirst. "They chased the doe down there. 'Twas too steep for me to climb down."

"And they didna have enough sense to know they'd have to haul her back up if they got her?"

"We wounded her," Kyle said. "'Twas our responsibility to dispatch her so she wouldna suffer."

"Good lads," Calum said, praising them for following a deer they'd injured rather than let it die slowly and in pain.

Ella shook her head, her gaze on Kyle as he returned her water skin to her, then she looked up at Calum. "What should we do?"

He didn't want to leave Ella alone out here, but her expression told him she didn't want the lad to wait much longer for the healer, either. "A ravine, ye said? How far is it?"

"I dinna ken. I've been limping along for a while."

"Let's find it, then I'll take ye back to the others. One of them can take ye to Mhairi and the rest can help us with the other lads."

He lifted Kyle onto his horse while Ella mounted hers, then he mounted behind the lad and followed the trail of broken brush and blood smears he had left. Before long, they got to the ravine.

"Georgie," Ella called out.

"We're down here," he answered. "Ye found us! We kenned ye would."

"Thank the saints," she said and traded a relieved smile with Calum.

"Do ye need help getting out of there?" Calum dismounted and walked to the edge, but it was getting too dark to see much down the slope.

"Aye," another lad answered. "We've got a deer."

"And enough blood, I'll wager, to attract every predator within miles," Calum muttered. "Move away from it," Calum told them, then turned to Ella and asked quietly, "Can this lad wait for Mhairi while we get these lads out of the hole they're in?"

"I dinna think so. He's lost some blood, Calum, and he's exhausted. I'm worried for him."

He huffed out a breath, torn between Kyle's safety and Ella's. But Ella's frown told him Kyle's need was more urgent. "I'll take him back to the others. I want ye to stay here."

"Very well." She glanced down the ravine.

"Right here," he repeated. "I dinna want ye going down there in the dark. If ye fall and hurt yerself, ye'll no' be able to help anyone else, and some of the other lads may need ye."

She gave him a distracted nod but didn't answer.

"Ella."

She frowned. "I hear ye. Stay here."

He rode back to their campsite as quickly as he could in the growing dark, ducking branches and folding his body over Kyle's as needed to keep him safe through the trees. "We found them," he announced when he arrived.

"Thank ye," Muireall told him, coming forward to grasp his hand before he could dismount. She frowned at the lad whose head slumped onto his chest, then up at Calum, who still used one arm to hold the lad upright. Then she looked around. "Where are the rest of them? And Ella? Is Georgie well?"

"Aye, so far as I ken, but Ella wants this lad sent back to Mhairi. Nora, ye will take him. He fell asleep on the way here. Or passed out. He's lost some blood. Tell Mhairi, and that Ella rinsed and checked his wounds before she wrapped them. The rest of ye will break camp and come with me."

Calum dismounted and transferred the lad to Nora's horse. Kyle didn't stir, which told Calum he'd passed out. Ella had been right to send him back to Mhairi and not wait for the others.

Nora mounted behind the lad and got a good grip around him to keep him from falling, then, wasting no time, told Calum, "Good hunting," before she rode away.

Calum was pleased to see that while he and Nora dealt with Kyle, the others had smothered their small campfire and gathered the supplies they'd set out to pass the night. Before long, they were ready.

"With me," Calum said, and led them back to where he'd left Ella at the edge of the ravine.

She was gone.

His heart dropped into his belly. Where was she? He called out, "Ella!"

When she didn't answer, he swore and let his horse find its way down the slope into the ravine. The others followed.

At the bottom, the scent of blood hit him first. The deer? Or were others hurt? Another thought stopped his breath. What if Ella had obeyed him and stayed on the rim? Alone up there, if anyone else found her, she'd have had no defense but to try to escape down here. Had raiders taken Ella and killed the lads? His whole body went cold. He should have taken her back to camp with him. He shook himself. Find the lads first.

When they found the deer, he realized the lads had done as he ordered and moved away from the carcass. They were alive, and God willing, Ella was with them. She had to be.

He would have been relieved to see her if she had followed his order to stay on the rim and wait. If she weren't so damned independent. But knowing her, since she knew one lad had been hurt, she probably couldn't resist the urge to come down to check on the others, and was with them now. She'd better be. He needed to get these lads out of here, not spend the rest of the night searching for her.

He shook his head and pushed the thought aside as he followed the lads' tracks, and the trail of broken branches they'd thoughtfully left behind.

Eventually, he came to a halt. He could hear voices, and the smells on the breeze told him the lads were near. And

Ella, damn her. As glad as he was that she was safe, his temper rose, too. She wasn't supposed to have risked the descent into the ravine in the dark. By herself.

He found them in a lean-to built from pine boughs stacked around a thick-girthed tree. Had she come up with that idea? "All right, everyone out," he commanded, still irritated with Ella, but proud of the foresight someone had used to protect the lads from the cold night air. Their initiative and skill impressed him.

"We kenned ye would find us," the first one out announced. Georgie. He spotted his sister behind Calum and ran to her horse.

"Who's idea was the shelter?" Calum asked as the rest crawled out after Ella. She stood, brushing pine needles from her clothes and pulling a few from her hair.

Calum was so relieved to see her safe that his fingers twitched with the need to help her. To touch her. Even better, to kiss her.

"The lads and I helped, but it was Georgie's idea," she told him as Muireall dismounted and wrapped her brother in a fierce hug. "We just did some of the work."

"Ye were supposed to stay on the rim," Calum reminded her.

"Georgie said one of the lads was hurt, so I let my sure-footed mount pick its way down," she told him, one eyebrow raised in challenge. "Liam has a twisted ankle, but he'll be fine in a fortnight or so." A happy smile lit her face as she let her gaze travel over the lads around her.

He hadn't expected he could be even more attracted to her than he already was. She wasn't afraid. She was glad to be here. Satisfied that she'd been able to help the two lads who'd needed her. She was showing him there was even more to sweet, shy Ella than he'd already given her recently revealed stubborn side credit for. She'd surprised him again.

"Then let's get them home." He gestured for the lads to mount up with the rest of his searchers. Georgie rode with his sister. Ella insisted on taking Liam with her.

"And dinna forget our deer," Georgie said.

Calum sighed. "Aye, and yer deer." His horse was largest, so the doe wound up tied behind his saddle, dripping blood the whole way back to the Brodie keep since he didn't want to take the time to tie it up in a tree, gut it and let the blood drain away. They were lucky that it started to rain as the Brodie keep came into view. The blood trail they left behind would soon wash away.

THAT EVENING, Ella told Mhairi about the boys' adventure and Muireall's pride in her brother's heroic actions. And how she'd probably confine him to the keep for the rest of his time fostering here. Or the rest of his life. He hadn't argued against tracking the doe they'd wounded, but he was the one who directed the lads to start breaking branches so they left an easy trail for Calum to follow. They knew he'd be out looking for them.

"How did Calum like having ye along and in his charge?"

Ella snorted. "No' very much at first. I think he saw me

more as a burden than someone to help. Until we found poor Kyle, or he found us." She glanced around at the sleeping lad. Mhairi insisted he stay in the herbal overnight so she could watch for fever. "And after Kyle led us to the rest, I discovered Liam had twisted his ankle." She crossed her arms. "I turned out to be useful after all." Liam was with his parents, his ankle wrapped and with orders to stay off it for the next few days.

"How did ye feel about being there? And caring for the lads away from the keep?"

Ella closed her eyes, thinking back over what happened since she'd joined Muireall and the others on their quest. "Terrified. At first. I thought Calum would insist I stay behind. But I wanted to be with him, in his world, so he'd see a different side to me than he did in here." She gestured at the space around them. "I worried that I would have to use my bow and arrows against raiders, and I wouldn't be good enough to protect myself, much less anyone else. Thankfully, that never happened."

"Nonetheless, ye are a brave lass to risk it," Mhairi told her as she finished putting the herbal to rights after taking care of Kyle's wounds and Liam's ankle. "Few would be able to do what ye did."

"I felt like I belonged. And I think I forced Calum to realize he doesna ken me as well as he thought." Muireall had been right. Going with him, seeing him do what he did best, while also showing him things she could do that he didn't expect, had felt good. If it opened a door in the wall between them, she would call it a good start. "But if I failed in that, it still felt good to care for the lads, even the little I could do out in the woods. I kenned ye would look after Kyle, and once I got back here, I would, too. Once we got them all back safely."

Ella smiled, then chuckled. "Ye shouldha seen Calum grumbling about having the lads' deer tied to his horse, dripping blood the whole way back here. He didna stop until the rain began."

"So, the lads were successful hunters!"

"Aye, they brought coneys and a deer back to Cook. I expect 'twas an adventure they'll no' soon forget."

Mhairi smiled sagely, her eyes bright and approving. "For ye, too, lass, aye?"

"I ken what ye are thinking," Ella told her. "I finally feel as though I fit in at Brodie. And with ye."

"Ye do, Ella. Ye have a place with me, caring for Brodie, if ye want it."

Ella gave her a tired smile. "I'm grateful ye want me here." But she still couldn't give Mhairi the assurance she wanted. Not until she knew if things would now be different—better—with Calum.

She went to bed, dreaming of Calum's change in attitude toward her. She'd seen the admiring looks he'd given her once he was sure she was safe. In her dream, he took her in his arms again and kissed her as he'd done in the hallway. But this time, they didn't argue. This time, they stumbled through his open door and into his chamber, then fell onto his bed, wrapped in each other's arms, kissing, touching, and exploring with more heat and passion than she believed possible in her life. Her arousal built quickly as his lips moved down her throat and his hands pulled at her skirts, seeking her burning flesh underneath.

Before her dream Calum could go further, pounding on her door woke her up. Her blood still raging in her veins, she wanted to cry. Instead, she got up, wrapped a shawl over her chemise and around her shoulders, and answered the door.

Kenneth stood there, looking grim as he stared over her head. "Euan's hurt," he told her. "They'll need ye."

Minutes later, dressed and downstairs, she heard raised voices coming from the bailey, and she ran all the way into the herbal to ready it.

Kenneth came in and lifted the sleeping Kyle from his cot. "I told Muireall. She'll be down soon. I'll see this lad safe somewhere else," he told her.

"Good thinking," Ella agreed. "Thank ye."

Mhairi arrived before Kenneth left with Kyle. She confirmed Ella's conclusion that the lad hadn't developed a fever, and let Kenneth carry him away.

Several men carrying Euan between them came in next. Euan's right arm, wrapped in a piece of Brodie plaid barely recognizable for the blood that soaked it, dripped blood off his fingers, leaving a trail of red on the stone flooring. The healer raised her voice. "Lay him down on the table, there. Good," she added when they got him settled the way she wanted. "Now, back up and stay out of my way, or leave. Ella and I will tend to him. Someone fetch Muireall."

"I'm here. Kenneth woke me." Euan's bride's voice cut through the rumble of concerned voices as Euan's men trailed out of the herbal, but only going as far as the hallway outside the chamber. "What happened?" She moved to Euan's side and took his good hand.

"I'm fine," Euan rasped softly, trying to sit up.

The healer, who had just uncovered the wound on his upper arm, pushed him back down. "Ye are no' fine. And ye will do as I say or—"

"Suffer the consequences. I ken it," Euan rasped.

She quirked her lips, giving him a brief smile, then gestured to Ella. "Ye ken what I need."

Ella nodded and fetched the pot of the herbal poultice to pack the wound, another of the tincture the healer used to prevent it from festering, cloth to wrap it, and wine to dull Euan's pain. If he didn't pass out, he would need it.

Ella poured a cup of wine and handed it to Muireall, then she and Mhairi helped him lift his head enough to swallow some of it.

Euan nodded his thanks as Muireall set the cup aside.

While the healer worked, Iain arrived, pushing through the men now clustered in the chamber's doorway. "What happened?" His demand silenced the low rumble of the men watching the healer work.

Euan tried to sit up again to answer his laird, but Mhairi pushed him down. "Now is no' the time, laird," she objected.

"Then someone else can fill me in. Euan wasna the only man there." He turned to the men determined to watch over Euan. "Well?"

One of his men stepped forward and described their encounter with a second band of raiders. "We had the ones Euan thought Calum found in our custody," the man said, "which left only a few of us to fight off the new band. Six more of them. They came out of the forest before we kenned they were there."

"Where are they now?" Iain's question cut through affirmative noises the men who fought the raiders added to the speaker's report.

"Dead, the lot of them," the man told him. "Including a few of the ones we'd rounded up who broke free and joined the fight. The rest should be in our dungeon cells by now."

"How was Euan hurt?"

"Three of the late arrivals went after him."

"Three?" Iain shook his head. "Damn, Euan. Trouble still follows ye."

Ella knew Calum would not be happy when he heard about this. But she was glad Iain had ordered him to stay behind. Could he have fought in a battle like the one they described? And survived? Or would he have wound up like Euan—or worse? She glanced at Muireall, sorry for her friend, but grateful Calum was here to avoid this fight, and to find the lost lads.

"Aye, well," the man continued, "it took longer than it should have for any of us to get to Euan. We were all fighting for our lives. The three on him kept driving him away from the rest of us. I finished off the man I was fighting and took out one of the men on Euan. Then another, but the third had time to do that before another of ours got him." He gestured toward the bloody arm the healer calmly worked on while Euan. Muireall kept a comforting hand on his good shoulder.

"How bad is it? Iain directed the question to the healer.

But his glance strayed to Ella, then Muireall, and Ella wondered if he thought Euan would be as difficult a patient as Calum had been. Or if he would heal faster. Ella continued handing the healer whatever she asked for, while sending Muireall encouraging smiles and nods. Muireall stood with the hand not touching Euan clenched in front of her waist, her face alternately pale and flushed. "Ye'd best sit down," Ella told her, worried that Muireall would faint from shock and the fear of seeing so much blood on her husband.

Iain put one of the healer's stools behind her and gently encouraged her onto it.

The healer glanced up at Iain. "'Tis bad enough he'll be with me for a while. Have ye seen enough, laird? Do ye have what ye need?"

"Aye."

"Then ye and ye men, get out and let us work."

Iain nodded and gestured for the others to precede him. At the door, he paused. "Keep me appraised," he ordered. When the healer nodded, never looking up, he left.

"Muireall, talk to yer man," the healer ordered. "Yer voice will soothe him."

Muireall pulled her stool closer to Euan's other side and began speaking softly.

Ella knew her friend's loving tones were the balm Euan needed more than the wine. Muireall and Euan were very much in love. While her friend's voice was tinged with concern, even fear, Ella could see the effort she made to hide her feelings, and to reassure Euan that all would be well. Ella hoped she was right. The wound sliced deeply into his upper arm muscles. He was probably fortunate not to have lost the arm completely. The healer worked quickly to stop the bleeding, pack the wound and wrap it, then she poured a generous measure of the tincture on the wrapping over the wound, soaking it. But Ella saw that Euan had a long struggle ahead of him to heal and regain his strength in that arm.

And such a wound, in his sword arm, might have the potential, like Calum's, to change the course of his life, and make fighting difficult if not impossible. Ella's heart broke for him, and for Muireall, who would face that future, whatever it might be, with him.

Like Ella had hoped to do with Calum. Would her friends face the same challenges? The same fears and heartbreaks? Nay, they were already married, happy in their union, and fully supported each other. Their situation was vastly different from hers with Calum. Muireall would be able to tend to her husband with no fear of him rejecting her help. And Euan would be glad of her devotion. Ella was certain of that.

Calum heard accounts of the battle with the raiders and Euan's wound the next morning. It was all the talk when he came down to the great hall to break his fast. With such news, especially so soon after he woke up, his appetite fled. Irritation filled his belly. Why had no one fetched him? He couldn't believe he had slept through the noise and commotion of their arrival. Muireall should have sent someone for him. How bad was Euan hurt? Calum didn't bother to sit down, but headed straight for the herbal.

Mhairi gave him a look when he showed his face in her door that warned him to go no further. She held a finger to her lips for silence, then shooed him away, waving with both hands.

He barely had a moment to glimpse Euan, lying pale and still on one of the cots, a sight that made his chest ache. Muireall curled in on herself on another cot next to her husband. Did she fear he wouldn't wake? How bad was his wound? He beckoned Mhairi to him. "How bad is it?"

She shrugged. "I've seen worse. He lost a lot of blood on the way here, which is why he looks the way he does. As long as he doesna succumb to fever, he'll be well in a few weeks."

"Weeks!"

"Aye, for the wound to heal and for him to regain his strength in that arm. Dinna fash, Calum. I'm watching him. Ella will, as well. And Muireall. At the first sign of trouble, we'll ken it and do what's needed. Now, go on with ye."

He did as she ordered. He returned to the great hall. Where was Georgie? Someone there would know.

Over an ale, bread and honey, and simple bowls of lamb and barley stew, Kenneth filled him in on what they'd faced rounding up the men Calum had found, and the surprise raid by the rest. "We were stretched too thin keeping your lot under control," Kenneth told him. "When the rest showed up, it became a fight for our lives, and worse when some of our prisoners broke free and joined their fellows against us." He related how Euan's injury happened and the rushed ride to get him back to the Brodie healer before his bleeding made him unable to stay on his mount.

"When we got here, Ella assisted the healer in cleaning and wrapping his wound. She and Muireall are close. They'll make sure Euan gets good care."

Calum listened with half an ear, guilt making him restless and heartsore. He should have been there with Euan. He found the raiders. He should have been part of the group to bring them in. One more sword might have kept Euan from being injured.

His muscles tensed with anger. Damn his eye. Damn the English sword that damaged it at Harlaw. And for what? Nothing! Domhnall had slunk away during the night, taking his forces with him—or most of them. Neither side could claim victory, though both had since done so. The battle had not settled the dispute over Ross territory. Nothing had been gained, yet he'd nearly lost his sight in one eye because of it, and other men died. He'd be damned if he'd lose Euan, too.

He should have been with him.

"I ken what ye're thinking," Kenneth told him. "But ye were needed here. I heard about the lads' hunting trip. Without ye here while we were gone, they might still be lost in the woods. Or worse."

Calum nodded, his mind immediately picturing Ella tending Kyle's injuries. Ella must be exhausted. She'd gone out with the search party, then dealt with Euan's injury during the night. Muireall, too. "Where is Georgie?"

Kenneth laughed. "Still confined to his chamber. I took Kyle up to stay with him after we brought Euan to the herbal. Cat is with them. Annie is keeping an eye on them, too."

Calum shoved the remainder of his food away and stood. "I'll go check on Euan."

Kenneth shook his head. "He was asleep when ye went by there before ye came here. It hasna been that long. He's probably still asleep. Best ye wait for the healer to tell us when he wakes."

Frustrated, Calum finished his meal, then headed outside to the practice ground. No one was out there yet, so he took advantage of the privacy to pick up a bow and work on his accuracy against the most distant target set up against the back wall. That kept him occupied until others started to show up. Including Iain.

"Spar with me," Iain offered once Calum emptied his quiver of arrows. He hefted his longsword.

Calum wasn't eager to let the laird test his recovery with no warning. He had no doubt Iain would use this session to judge whether, or how soon, to let him go out with a fighting force. But since Iain was standing in front of him with an expectant look in his eye and a tight grip on the hilt, Calum didn't have much choice. Spar with him now, or make Iain think he wasn't ready yet and wouldn't be for weeks more. He nodded, collected his arrows from the target and put everything away for someone else to use, then chose a longsword from the supply kept in the nearby weapons shed next to the smithy.

"How's yer left side?"

Calum appreciated Iain asking instead of just swinging at him from that side and seeing if he had the wherewithal to duck or defend against a blow. "Better. No' yet perfect. I expect ye to challenge me, but will thank ye to do it without taking off my head."

Iain grinned. "I'll do my best to leave it on yer shoulders."

They started slowly, warming up and letting their muscles loosen. As the pace picked up, Calum began to enjoy himself, especially when attacking or defending straight on or to his right. His left side was more of a challenge, his vision still a little blurry, but the peripheral vision that he depended on to be aware of what was coming at him from that side seemed intact. He never missed seeing Iain's blade arcing toward him from that direction, and was aware when Iain pulled up short to avoid hurting him, but by then, Calum's blade was in place to block Iain's attack.

Even better, he challenged Iain's defense more and more as they continued.

Finally, Iain dropped his sword point to the ground, calling a halt.

"I canna tell that ye have any problem seeing on yer left side," Iain told him. "Ye did very well."

"Thank ye. And thank ye for the practice. 'Tis true. I always kenned where yer blade was."

"If Mhairi agrees, I think ye are ready to rejoin the warriors in addition to yer scouting duties."

"'Tis good news, laird. Thank ye."

"Thank Mhairi and Ella, Calum, for their care of ye. And yer own persistence."

Calum nodded. "I'll talk to Mhairi today." And Ella? He did owe Mhairi his thanks. Ella, too, though that would be harder to deliver. Despite how well they got on rescuing the lost lads, after their kiss and the argument that followed it, she might not care to hear what he had to say on the subject of her care of his eye.

Iain slapped him on the back and left the practice field. Calum stood for a moment, watching him go, absorbing what had just happened. While he'd been bedridden, how he'd dreamed of this day, and feared it would never come. Now, he felt determined. Vindicated. Relieved and happy. He left the field before anyone else noticed him loitering and started rumors about what Iain might have said to him. He'd get cleaned up and talk to Mhairi, then get something to eat. If she gave her permission, he planned to ask Iain about joining the next scouting mission to make sure all the raiders had been arrested or driven from Brodie and its allies' territory. He no longer needed to fear getting into a fight, or letting down the men he fought with.

"I've enough men in the field," Iain told him after the evening meal as they shared a cup of wine in his solar to celebrate Mhairi's approval. "Until we ken more from them, and from our allies, I am reluctant to risk any more scouts—especially ye. I will give it a few more days for everyone to report back. We'll ken more then. And Calum," he added and paused.

"Aye?"

"Ye did well today with a blade. This is naught to do with ye. I dinna want to risk anyone right now."

Disappointed, but unable to argue with Iain's logic, Calum bid his laird a good eve.

"Another thing," Iain said, stopping Calum as he rose to leave.

"Aye?"

Iain looked as though he was considering whether to continue with whatever came to his mind, or to dismiss him.

He leaned forward and met Calum's questioning gaze with a look that made Calum uneasy.

"I've been meaning to talk to ye about something else. Ella has done well in her year with us. And she was indispensable in caring for the lads when ye found them. She's grown in confidence and in skills she didna possess when she first arrived here. And those make her even more attractive to other men, ye ken? I have heard rumblings from some of the men here—no' directly, mind ye—that lead me to think 'twould be best for her to be married soon. Or at least, betrothed, before something happens that none of us, least of all Ella, will like.

Calum couldn't believe what he was hearing. She was at risk from within their own clan? Being betrothed, or even wed, would not guarantee her safety if someone within their walls chose to accost her. "What would ye have me do?"

"I ken the two of ye are friends, but Ella has the kind of beauty to attract attention wherever she goes. And she doesna have a husband to protect her."

"She has a clan. This one."

"Brodie men are still men. They see her, and they see that in a year with her, ye have no' claimed her, despite yer obvious interest in her. By now, ye've convinced them ye'll never be more than friends with her. And when she leaves the keep, as she has and will again, on an errand, or to help someone, or for a gathering of clans, there will be more men to covet her."

Calum clenched his teeth. He didn't like hearing this from anyone, least of all Iain, whom he knew to be observant, fair, and at his wife's behest, occasionally meddling. "I've been giving her time."

"'Tis noble of ye."

Noble? Calum didn't think of himself that way. But there was no sarcasm in Iain's tone. He meant it. Calum nodded, accepting the compliment.

"But time is exactly what ye may be running out of," Iain continued. "Think on that, and on what ye want from her. For her, as well as for yerself, Calum. If she is accosted, I'll have to act. If I receive a betrothal offer for her, ye ken I will have to consider it, and give Ella the choice of whether to accept it or no'."

Calum stared at the wall behind Iain's head, unable to find words. He didn't know what Iain's warning made him feel. Fear? Surely not. Dismay, possibly. Urgency? If Iain's goal was to make him uneasy, it worked. But why try to force him to make a decision now, after all he'd been through? This conversation did have the feel of Annie's work. Perhaps she'd heard about their kiss from Muireall or even directly from Ella, as well as the argument and hard feelings that came after it. Though they'd done well together saving the lads, they hadn't spent much time together since then. Did that also have something to do with this? Was Iain's characterization true, that they'd never be more than friends? The idea made Calum's belly ache.

"Very well," Iain said, relenting when Calum didn't respond. "Go and think on what I've said."

Calum nodded again, stood, and left, closing the solar door behind him. He took a few paces toward the great hall, then changed his mind. He needed to think, but on his own. He couldn't deal with Iain's meddling right now.

He went to the herbal to check on Euan. Muireall would be there. Perhaps she could help him decide what to do about what Iain told him. A woman's perspective. Almost Ella's. Muireall knew her best.

Muireall sat with her sleeping husband when Calum arrived.

"How is he?" He asked softly, reluctant to disturb his friend.

"Resting well," Muireall said, rising to join him at the door to the herbal. "The healer will decide in a day or two about moving him back to our chamber. For now, she wants to keep him close in case he develops a fever."

"And Georgie? How are he and the lads now they're back?"

"Iain had a stern talk with the lot of them about leaving without permission or any adults to escort them. They could have died..." Her voice choked, and she took a breath. "But they didna. Thanks to ye finding them."

"And thanks to Georgie keeping his head and making a safe place for them to pass the night, though I'm glad in the end, they didna need it."

"Iain congratulated them on the things they did right and said he's adding direction finding to their training, starting immediately. And he told them that they're all confined to the keep until we're certain the raiders are out of the area."

"That could be weeks," Calum pointed out, feeling sorry

for the lads, especially after the way he'd been confined, though for very different reasons.

"Aye, it could. I dinna think the men with Euan are certain they got all the raiders ye found. Or that they're the only ones still out there."

Calum hung his head. "I regret that I wasna there to help defend him," Calum told her.

Muireall shook her head. "Ye are no' to blame. He was outnumbered and unlucky. Thankfully, our men got him back quickly and the Brodie healer is excellent at her craft. He will recover, if slowly. Regaining his strength and full use of his arm will come, but with pain."

Calum studied the sleeping man. His best friend looked wan and tired even as he rested. Had he looked the same before he woke up after Harlaw? Did Ella sit with him as Muireall now did with Euan, worrying and wondering if the healer's assurances would come to pass?

Seeing what Muireall was going through made him feel like his rejection of Ella's help had been even more unfair to her than he'd suspected. Possibly, he had saved her hours of worry, watching him sleep, waiting for his next breath, and wondering if he would ever see with two eyes and be able to fight to protect her like the warrior he used to be. But Ella was enough like Muireall that he now saw she would not have wanted to be anywhere else but with him. Even as Janet, risking his ire, she did what she thought best for him.

He'd been an arse.

He took Muireall's hand and squeezed it gently. "If there is aught ye need, aught I can do, ye have only to ask."

She gave him a tired smile that did not quite reach her eyes. "I ken it. Thank ye, Calum. Euan will be grateful, too."

Calum pursed his lips, unsure what to say. This was not the time to seek her advice. But she had given him clarity without his asking. Instead of answering, he dropped her hand, nodded and took his leave.

TWO DAYS LATER, after the healer cleaned his wound and stitched it closed, she agreed to let Euan move from the herbal to his own bed. His and Muireall's. Just getting him up the stairs exhausted him, even with Kenneth and two of Mhairi's lads to help. Ella sat for an hour with Muireall while her husband slept, silently lending support and companionship she knew Muireall needed while Georgie was on the training ground with Iain and Kenneth and the other lads. All the fears that plagued Calum while his eyes were covered now weighed heavily on her friend—and his. And where was Calum? She didn't think he'd visited Euan in the herbal. Muireall would have told her if he'd come during her absences. His absence was out of character for him and his friendship with Euan. His best friend and partner was injured. Where had he been?

But Calum arrived as Ella left Euan and Muireall's chamber. She nodded to him as they passed each other in the doorway, but he only glanced at her before stepping inside.

Annoyed at his slight, she paused outside the door after Calum entered, unsure of his mood, and concerned that his arrival would disturb Euan's rest. But Calum stood, silently, regarding his friend, a frown knitting his brow. "I thought he'd be better by now," he said so softly that Ella nearly missed it.

After a glance at Ella, Muireall greeted him in a low voice. "Ye can see he is resting," she told Calum. "Much as ye did while ye recovered. 'Tis best if ye dinna wake him." She kept her gaze on Calum and waited for his reply.

"I owe ye both an apology," he said. "I've been reluctant to help Euan after the fuss I made while under the healer's care," Calum admitted in a voice as soft as Muireall's, "but he's my best friend. I would never abandon him—or ye, lass—but I have to admit it took me a while to get past my own reluctance."

"Ye went through a long and difficult healing," Muireall told him. "'Tis understandable that ye would hesitate to spend much time in the herbal. Now that he's up here, ye can visit more often."

"Ye give me too much grace, lass. I can be as selfish and as proud as any man. More than most. But Euan will get better. I will do all I can to help."

Ella noticed Euan stirring and faded back from the door so he wouldn't spot her beyond Calum. What would Calum think to know she was back here, listening to every word he said?

"There isna much either of us can do but get through what has befallen us," Euan muttered, clearly having heard at least some of what Calum said to Muireall. "Yer eye may never be the same. My arm may never be as strong, or as fast and battle-ready. We are what we have become, aye?"

Calum shook his head, stepped forward, and placed a hand on Euan's good shoulder. "Come on, man. We canna let this destroy us. We will do the work and regain what we once had. Together. I will help ye, just as ye helped me."

Ella's heart lifted to hear a note of optimism in his voice, even if it was only for Euan's sake. She hoped he believed what he was telling his friend. Helping Euan would help him, too.

Should she go back into the chamber? If apologizing to Muireall and speaking to Euan helped improve Calum's mood and his acceptance of what he must overcome, how would he react to her presence? Would he apologize to her for how he'd treated her? They'd seemed much like the way they used to be while searching for the lads. More comfortable with each other. Easier, companionable. But since they'd been back and Euan had been injured, it seemed the distance between them widened again. She'd been busy helping Mhairi and Muireall. But she had reason to hope. The four of them were close as friends until Calum's injury. The last few days convinced her they could be again.

She could ignore how he'd dismissed her presence when he arrived a few minutes ago. At that moment, his thoughts had been clearly focused on his friend, full of concern that Euan was not sitting up, but slept on like one dead, or nearly so. She would do as Muireall had done and give him at least that much grace.

Resolved, she moved to the doorway. When she stepped back into the chamber, as if she'd gone away and returned, Euan's gaze cut to her, alerting Calum. He turned, and for the first time since they'd returned from bringing home the lost lads, he gave her an honest smile, one that softened and reached his eyes, as though he finally realized, now that he saw a similar situation with his friend, why she had done for him what she did. And the forgiveness he'd proffered earlier with a generous helping of reluctance now seemed genuine. But could she count on it to last?

❦

FOUR DAYS LATER, Calum was happy to see Euan out of his chamber as he slowly approached Calum and Kenneth at their table in the great hall. "'Tis about time ye joined us," Calum told him as he sat down with a sigh.

"Aye," Kenneth added, "ye've been abed long enough. Ye have much to do."

"Dinna remind me," Euan said, frowning. "But this binding of the healer's prevents most anything I would like to do, including starting to train again."

"All in good time," Calum told him, doubting he yet had the strength to walk to the training ground, much less to lift a blade. "Take it from one who kens well the healer's mind. She willna let ye do more damage to that arm in yer haste to recover from yer injury."

"Which brings me to a conundrum of mine," Euan said, his gaze on Kenneth. "I canna do the job Iain gave me to do. Someone must take over training the younger lads." He shifted to study Calum. "Someone like ye."

"Me?" Calum's gaze shifted to Kenneth. Why not him or one of the other warriors? "I'm only just approved to begin training with blades myself. How can I do that for anyone else?"

"Aye, ye," Kenneth said, ignoring his question. "Euan, 'tis a good idea." He turned to Calum. "While ye train the lads, ye'll also be training yerself, aye?"

"Will I? Or will I end up battered by lads barely out of swaddling because I still canna see as well as I should on my left side."

"And what will ye do to compensate for that, I wonder?" Euan grinned. "Aye, a brilliant idea."

Calum frowned as he thought about Euan's idea. Despite how his friend looked after coming downstairs, Calum could see that he was regaining a good deal of his strength and energy. Muireall had already complained that it made him restless and quarrelsome. But Calum took it as a good sign that he was thinking about his responsibilities to the clan and how to meet them. And still thinking about how to help Calum progress. "I'll do it," he said, "so long as ye stay nearby to observe and help train. And to keep the wee monsters from doing too much damage to me, not to mention to each other."

Kenneth nodded. "Then we have a plan with several good outcomes. Iain will be pleased to hear about this.

Calum pursed his lips. All he needed was Iain observing the training in time for him to mess something up. "Why no' give this idea a few days to see how it goes before getting the laird involved, aye?"

"Verra well, I willna say anything to him," Kenneth promised. "But ye ken he's likely to be where he can see what's happening. Or someone else will tell him. Ye dinna have more than a day or so to decide how ye want to do this."

It took less time than that for Calum to realize he enjoyed both the training and the zest the young lads gave to everything they were asked to do. He demonstrated techniques for the lads to repeat, much as he'd been taught at that same age. Euan sat nearby, watching and offering suggestions. Kenneth dropped by for a few minutes, but apparently liked what he saw and went on his way.

Calum was in no real danger from the wooden swords the younger lads used—he gained a few bruises at worst. But he also found that trying to pay attention to what all the lads were doing all the time made him use his eyes more fully and within days, his reflexes were stronger and faster, his peripheral vision sharper, and he noticed improvements in himself all around.

Now if he could only say the same for his relationship with Ella.

CHAPTER 10

"Iain and Euan are ignoring reality."

The male voice drifting up from the bailey to Calum's open window stole his attention from the repair he was doing on the leather straps of his cotun before he had to don it and leave for the practice ground and his young charges there. Today would be their first chance to use dulled metal swords. The leather garment, tightly packed with woolen stuffing, acted as a light form of armor that would protect at least part of him from the worst of their wild swings.

The man's statement piqued his curiosity. What reality were Iain and Euan ignoring? Calum stood and moved silently closer to the window, hoping to overhear more.

"Aye, he's never going to be the scout he was," another man replied.

Calum's blood turned to ice. They were talking about him?

"Bloody blind man," the first agreed. "There are other men more qualified to do that job."

"Like us," his companion asserted. "With two good eyes and more sense than Calum ever had. Ye ken he went with Euan to Ross to get Eduard back. They barely got away with their lives."

That was pure shite. Calum's arm had been broken when their fishing boat, the Tangie, wrecked in a storm on a Ross cove. Euan also survived, found him and kept him alive. When he and Euan escaped in a small Ross boat with Muireall and the body they'd found washed up on the sand of their youngest crew member, he could only row with one hand. She'd had to help him with his oar to balance Euan's powerful strokes so they wouldn't go in circles.

Calum would have been of no use on Eduard's rescue mission, and didn't go. But the men who went, led by Euan, were successful.

Sudden rage heated his blood to boiling. Ignoring stealth in his fury, he stomped to the window and leaned out, determined to see who was speaking. But the men had moved on, and enough people milled around the bailey to make identifying his detractors impossible. Damn it. He needed to know who they'd been, and whether there were any more who thought the same way.

Despite Mhairi allowing him to go back to training and doing anything else Iain needed, he couldn't ignore the fact that his vision was still not exactly what it used to be, and its improvement was progressing more slowly than he hoped. If he had enough detractors like those two, would they be able to convince Euan and Kenneth, or even

Iain, to set him aside? To consign him to training others alone, no longer a scout or a warrior? All the fears that tormented him while his eyes were still bandaged came roaring back. None of it was true. He was doing well, and better every day. He could fight any man. Neither Euan nor Kenneth put pressure on him to find another path, another role to play in the clan. He didn't expect Iain would, either, without their support and recommendation.

But how did one fight rumors, falsehoods and mean-spirited jealousy? Who in Brodie would be so petty as to deny him the role he'd earned and excelled at for years?

Fists clenched, he glared out the window, searching, but there were too many pairs and groups of men moving about to be certain of anything, and the voices had been pitched low enough to keep passersby from understanding what was being said, so he hadn't recognized them. Not without a doubt. He could think of as many as six men with similar sounding voices that they might have been.

He should have given in to the urge and looked out the window sooner. Perhaps if they saw him staring down at them, they'd think twice about how qualified he was to be a Brodie scout.

He was about to turn away from the window when he heard a voice he did recognize. Ella's.

"Who do ye think ye are?" She sounded furious. "He's twice the man as the two of ye put together. How dare ye."

She was defending him? What had she heard? The two men must have continued talking about him as they moved away. He rushed back to the window to see whom she was confronting, but didn't see her. She must be around the corner of the tower, somewhere out of his view.

One of the men laughed and if he hadn't been certain Ella could tell him whom she confronted, he wouldn't have cared. It didn't matter. He recognized that cackle. He knew them now. Those men were two of the worst fighters the clan had. Euan kept them on the wall on guard duty, certain they'd be killed within moments in a hand-to-hand fight. Euan and Kenneth would be amused—and angry— when they heard about this.

Calum ceased being outraged over their comments. Instead, he listened for Ella's voice, but apparently, she'd made her point and moved on. And the two men had moved on as well. He heard no snide comments coming from them about her defense of him.

She'd defended him. Despite all he'd said and done to her, she cared.

How many times would he be reminded how wrong he'd been about her? How unfair?

ELLA'S daily routine often took her past the practice field, but today, she went another way. The smile Calum gave her in Euan's chamber made her hope they were getting past the barriers between them. But days passed since then, and he'd yet to take her aside to speak to her, much less to offer any companionship. The distance between them continued to frustrate her. Perhaps he'd been right that they didn't suit. She hadn't pictured a deadline when the healer suggested that if Calum no longer returned her affections, she might resort to finding someone else to give her what she needed. She'd thought they'd had a breakthrough, but apparently she'd been wrong.

So why had she defended Calum to those two oafs she'd overheard disparaging him? She knew why. She couldn't tolerate the tone of their comments, nor the fact that none of them were true, especially what they'd said about the rescues Brodie men made at Ross. Calum had been injured then, and unable to go with them. Aye, he still had much to overcome, but he was making great progress and he was still a better warrior—and a better man—than either of those two wastrels.

She was so deeply into her own thoughts that she ran into a wall of muscle before she realized there was someone in her way. She gasped and looked up. "Iain! I'm so sorry. I wasna watching where I was going." Of all people, she had to bump into the laird? What must he think of her?

"Dinna fash, lass," he told her as he steadied her, her upper arms wrapped in his large and capable hands. "Actually, we are well met. There is aught I wish to discuss with ye. Will ye come to my solar when ye finish the errand that brought ye this way?"

"Of course." What other answer could she possibly give the laird? "I can come now, if ye wish."

"Nay, lass. Take yer time. I'm going to observe how the wee lads are doing under Calum's instruction, then I'll return."

Ella nodded, but her belly tensed. Calum would not be

happy to see Iain watching him. Still, it had to happen sometime, and she couldn't think of a good reason to delay Iain.

"Good, Ella. Just…have a care where ye are going, aye?"

His grin told her he was teasing, not rebuking her. She smiled and went on her way, her thoughts now centered on what Iain might want to discuss with her. She hadn't noticed any air of seriousness or concern. It must be something simple, perhaps something for the healer or to prepare for the next feast day. Well, she'd find out soon enough.

She finished her errands and stopped by Iain's solar, but he wasn't back yet. Poor Calum. She was certain by now he was well aware the laird watched the training. She hoped all went well. She almost wished she'd gone her usual way and been at the training ground in time to see Iain's arrival there. And Calum's reaction. Iain could have summoned her from there.

Instead of entering the solar and taking a seat there to wait for him, she went back to the great hall. She'd see him when he came in, and he could let her know if he wanted some time to himself before meeting with her or not.

A few minutes later, Iain came in and gestured for her to join him as he walked to the solar.

Desperate for something to say, Ella asked the only thing she could think of. "How was the training?"

Iain glanced her way before speaking. Was he assessing whether her interest was truly in the training, or in Calum?

"Very good," he finally said, "The wee lads are making

excellent progress with Calum's help, and I see that Calum himself is improving, too."

"'Tis what Euan hoped to gain for his friend," Ella replied, pleased that Iain seemed satisfied. Calum, too, she was certain, or he would have been reluctant to take on the responsibility that Euan so ably carried out before he was hurt.

Iain gestured her to a seat at the worktable that took up part of the solar, then took a seat opposite her, but didn't say anything for several moments.

His hesitation made her heart begin to beat faster. Perhaps he had something more serious in mind after all.

"Have ye given any thought to what ye'd like yer own future to be, lass?"

Ella's belly clenched. "What do ye mean, laird?"

"Ye work closely with the healer and should consider becoming her apprentice. I ken she's asked ye to think on it. Before his injury, ye and Calum seemed to wish to be together. Is that still yer wish?"

Chills ran down Ella's arms and her throat seemed frozen. She couldn't get a word out, even if she knew how to answer Iain's question. Was that still her wish? So much depended on Calum. On his wishes, too. "I...I dinna ken. Calum and I have no'..." She trailed off, unsure how to describe what they were to each other.

"'Twill be yer decision, Ella," Iain said as if sensing the reason for her hesitation. "And if what seemed to be yer path in the past is no longer what ye want, I have another option ye might wish to consider."

"Another option?"

Iain gave her a reassuring smile and leaned forward. "I spoke to Calum about the possibility of a betrothal offer for ye in the future." What? Iain knew about her past. Surely he would not entertain a betrothal offer from someone she didn't know. He had to think she would reject it. Why would he put her in a position to go through that again?

He held up a hand as she, too, leaned forward, ready to object. "Dinna fash. I dinna have one. But I might have left him with the impression that I expected one could come at any time. From within Brodie, or from elsewhere. Annie has been telling me 'tis time for the two of ye to stop, as she put it, dancing around each other. I dinna mean to force ye into anything, lass. I simply want ye to think about what it is ye want," he said. "Because I hope Calum is doing the same."

He'd talked to Calum? Ella's breath froze in her chest. Her mind spun. What if an offer did come for her. Would it likely be from a Rose lad she'd met? Another Brodie? Someone at Sutherland? Someone she liked well enough to consider seriously? Or truly a stranger? It would be better if she knew the man, if only a little. Iain would know a stranger would be too easy for her to refuse. So, probably a Brodie. Could she do that to Calum? Marry another within the clan and force him to see her all the time? How would she feel if she remained here, and he married another? Nay, she couldn't fathom how she would live with that. She looked up at Iain, embarrassed again. His smile told her he'd noticed her woolgathering and waited for her to return her attention to him.

"Iain, I…" She choked to a halt. "Ye ken Calum hasna been himself since…"

"Everyone does, lass."

"I've done what I could for him."

"I ken ye have. No one blames ye for what Calum has gone through, or for how he's dealing with it. Or not dealing with it. Ye ken I wouldna bring this to ye if I had any qualms about ye and Calum together," Iain said. "I havena forgotten yer history, or how he has pursued ye, with care and concern for ye. Like Calum, I wouldna see ye forced to do anything ye dinna wish to do—openly and gladly. For that reason, I think ye must also consider whether marrying away from Brodie would make ye happy, or if ye would prefer to stay here."

"I must think on this," she told him when she was certain she understood the offer he made. He wouldn't force her into anything. Her fate was still hers to decide. "How much time…?"

"I said I willna force ye into anything ye dinna want. I meant it. Ye will take the time ye need."

"Thank ye, laird," she said and stood to go, wanting nothing more than to bolt from this chamber and forget the conversation they'd just had.

"Ella—" he said as she turned for the door.

She took a breath, forcing herself to calm down. "Aye, laird?"

"Let me also say that I would hate to see ye leave Brodie," Iain told her.

She nodded without turning back to face him and kept going. As she reached the doorway, his words echoed in her ears. She had made a home here, first as Muireall's companion, then helping the healer, all while nurturing a relationship with Calum that they both seemed to cherish. Until he was hurt.

Was this really home? As she hurried to her chamber where she could sit in silence and think, she looked around her at the people, the stones and timbers that made up the keep, the hearth that everyone gathered around, the touches that made a hall and a keep a home. But was it hers? Had it ever been? After helping to save the lost lads, she'd told Mhairi she finally felt like she belonged here, but Iain had just splintered the comfortable sense of security she'd achieved.

She might soon have little choice but to consider and possibly accept a betrothal offer—to stay or to go. She knew of no other options save the one Iain just gave her. She wanted no other options. Only Calum.

But, other than one kiss that had less to do with her than with celebrating his own success, or even with punishing her, Calum had given her no indication he still wanted to be with her. He'd been civil, but not yet as friendly as he used to be. Still, she had to believe they'd made some progress toward each other during the lads' rescue. Perhaps when Calum took some time to reflect on what Iain said to him, he'd be forced to realize that if he didn't soon make up his mind, he could lose her forever.

Calum couldn't fathom how long it took for Iain's conversation with Ella to get back to him. Mhairi pulled no punches when she told him about it. "Dinna blame me," she complained. "I just found out today. Ella kept it to herself while she thought about what Iain told her."

"For a ten-day?"

"Apparently. Ye ken she's a deep one."

"Did she say whether she'd decided anything?"

"Ye are a fool, Calum. She's waiting for ye. She's waited for ye for nigh on a year. How long do ye think ye can treat her like this?" She didn't hide her disgust, but Calum suspected her dismay had as much to do with the idea of Ella marrying away from Brodie so that Mhairi lost her assistant and prospective apprentice as it did with Calum's failures.

And as for Iain and probably Annie, too, they were meddling where they were not welcome. He needed to tell them so. Iain, anyway. He could tell his wife. Calum would be happy to leave that unpleasant chore to him.

Calum left Mhairi and went straight to Iain's solar.

"I canna believe ye would offer Ella a betrothal to someone else," Calum raged at him after he stormed in and closed the door behind him, still smarting from hearing the news.

"Who told ye that?"

"Mhairi, when I saw her a few minutes ago about my eye. She said ye told Ella she had choices, and that she might be in a position to decide her future soon. With someone else. Another clan. When ye posed this to me, ye didna also tell me ye were going to plant this poisonous seed in Ella's mind. Damn it, do ye want her to leave? I thought ye understood that I want her—when she's ready."

"I spoke to ye nearly a fortnight past," Iain reminded him, not backing down. "What have ye done since then?"

He waited while Calum sputtered, fighting for something to say to absolve himself, but nothing came out.

"Calum, there are many men interested in a lass as lovely and kind as Ella. Honorable men, who would treat her well. Surely there are several who would care for her— even love her—for her whole life. Such a match would be good for both of them. Or for both of ye."

Calum groaned at that. "Ye ken I care for her. And ye ken how shy she is around strangers. Do ye seriously expect her to accept as another husband a man she doesna ken?"

"She kens many good men. No' well. No' as well as she kens ye, for instance."

How serious was Iain about this? And how soon? "Who are ye thinking about?"

"I willna tell ye, no' with ye in this frame of mind. Ye'll run off and start a clan war."

"Give me a little credit, Iain."

"If ye are so fashed about this, why have ye no' offered for her yerself?"

"I told ye before, I was giving her time…"

"Ye've given her long enough. And by dragging this out for a year, treating her as ye have since ye were hurt, ye ken fine that ye've hurt her, perhaps worse than Thomas Ross ever did."

That stung. And the blade bit deep. But Iain was right. He'd been a fool. A proud and stupid fool.

"I have a claim on her. Unspoken, aye, but what I feel for her is…between us." And now he even sounded like a fool. But he hadn't admitted to himself what he felt for Ella. He certainly would not tell Iain.

Iain grinned and waved toward the door, a clear invitation for Calum to leave. "Then ye must convince her, no' me."

Could he? He hadn't done so well in his last conversations with her. If he meant to repair the damage Iain pointed out, correctly, that he'd done, he was going to have to impress her. But how?

ELLA WAITED IMPATIENTLY in the keep's garden, pacing among the roses she hadn't the wit to stop to enjoy. She was distantly aware of the cloud of scent around her, something she would normally savor, but Calum's request, delivered by Muireall, that she meet him here had set her pulse to racing and her mind to spinning. Her friend would not tell her what he wanted. Perhaps she could not because Calum had not told her, but simply requested she deliver his message. Muireall would have done so without question, knowing Ella's feelings for the man, and hoping as Muireall always did, for something good to come from his unusual request.

But what would she consider a good outcome? Had he learned from Mhairi or Muireall that Iain spoke to her much as she knew he'd already spoken to Calum? Was that why he was eager to speak to her in the relative privacy of the walled garden?

At one time she thought Calum the only man who would ever make her happy in this life. But much had changed. And not enough had changed.

Or had it?

What did she want? Iain's surprising advice confused her. Had Annie put him up to this? How would she know? Annie would not reveal something Iain held close. Iain all but said she should stay at Brodie. She was certain they would want her to stay with Calum, too. So did she.

Ella feared any decision that would take her to a strange place and a strange man. She belonged at Brodie. With Calum. She could admit that now. To herself, at least.

Calum came through the gate and closed it behind him, then turned and stopped when he saw her.

He just looked at her, and Ella could not interpret the

expression on his face. Sadness? Fear? Hope? She couldn't discern whether it boded well or ill for whatever he intended to say to her.

She studied him in return. He hadn't changed on the outside. Still the tall, handsome warrior who pursued her once she and Thomas Ross had repudiated each other. Calum did not care about her past. He cared about her. Or she thought he did. Had it all been simply that he wanted her, as a man wants a woman he thinks he cannot have? Lust, not love?

What did she see in his eyes now?

She tried a small smile, hoping he would respond in kind.

He didn't, but he took a step toward her. "Thank ye for agreeing to meet me, Ella. I ken I have been hard on ye. Unfair, even, in my condemnation of yer actions."

His voice was soft. Gruff. The pain in his eyes had not abated, and Ella's body chilled as if ice filled her veins instead of hot blood. What was he leading up to?

"There is so much I need to say to ye," he continued when she didn't respond. "To apologize for. To ask ye. I dinna ken where to start, save to say that I ken I hurt ye. I've been an arse since I woke up from Harlaw. I felt sorry for myself and let self-pity overtake every other important thing in my life. Including ye. I never meant to hurt ye. And I canna begin to explain to ye how deeply sorry I am."

He was apologizing. But why? Was he telling her goodbye? Ella fought the twisting pain climbing like a vining rose, thorns scraping from her belly to her chest, and found her voice. "I accept yer apology, Calum." It was all she could do.

He seemed to relax a wee after she spoke. Perhaps this would not be as bad as she'd feared.

"Ye once told me ye wanted back what we had before I was injured. Can ye accept that I want that, too?"

Heat rose, thawing the ice in her veins and melting some of the thorns twisting in her chest. But she didn't yet trust where this conversation was going. "I have hoped for that."

"Am I too late? I ken Iain spoke to ye about yer future. Ours. Mine, too. I treated ye badly. Ella or Janet, both. I like both sides of ye. I want ye to be able to be yerself around me, Ella and Janet combined."

"Do ye?" Ella straightened her back and met his gaze, drawing strength from within herself. She was tired of waiting for him to get to the point. "Have ye come to this realization only because Iain and Annie have decided to push us toward each other? Are ye begging my forgiveness? Or letting me go with kindness by blessing a possible union between me and another man, as Iain suggested? What do *ye* want, Calum?"

"I want what we had. And more. I want the future we once hoped to have together."

He paused and Ella watched him, wide-eyed, not yet sure if she believed what she heard. He sounded like the old Calum, the man she had begun to fall in love with. Before he'd been injured and became angry and impossible. "I have wanted that, too," she answered, daring to admit that truth despite the risk of what Calum might do with it.

"But I want more than that," he said. "I want ye to ken how I feel about ye. I want to say to ye the things I never had the courage to say, before now." He took another step closer. "I was blind. Not my eyes." He prodded his chest with stiff fingers. "In here. And too proud. And foolish. But I've learned my lesson. Aye, Iain and Annie's meddling opened my eyes, but so did ye. I see ye, Ella Munro. No' just yer beautiful face. I see the good in ye, I see how ye care for others. I finally see that I canna bear to go through life without ye at my side. I see how much ye love me, no matter how ye try to hide it. But most of all, I see how much I have hurt ye and I regret every moment of pain that I caused ye. And I never want to do that again. I love ye, Ella, more than I ken how to tell ye."

"Calum…" She'd never imagined she'd hear those words from his lips. She reached out to him, but he didn't move to take her hand.

"Let me finish, love. I want to show ye how much I love ye. For ye to see that I mean it. To see how much ye mean to me. Ye are everything to me, Ella. I dinna ken how better to tell you than to say I'd rather be blind again that to go through life without ye. I want ye to marry me, lass."

"Calum!" This time she gasped his name and held up a hand. "Ye would rather be blind? How can ye say something like that after what ye have been through?" And how could she consider, even for a moment, wedding anyone else after he made a declaration like that. With all the rest of what he said. She couldn't look away from him, over-whelmed by the entreaty in his voice and on his face.

"I say it to make ye understand how real this is. How sincere I am. How much I love ye, Ella. All of ye."

"I must...I canna..." Her heart was bursting. Not in sadness, but from fullness. It could not contain all the feelings Calum's surprising admission, his declaration of love and offer of marriage, made her feel. Her heart would shatter, and she'd die right in front of him. She couldn't let that happen.

Stymied by her own emotions, unable to speak, she turned and blindly ran from him. She thought he followed her, but after a few steps, he stopped. She almost stopped, too, when she reached the garden's gate, but something drove her on. She needed to think, to get control of herself. To make sure the decision she made was the right one for her—and for him. She would not let herself be forced into anything, not by Iain, and not even by Calum's heart-rending profession of love for her. But, oh, how sweet his words had been. She couldn't doubt his sincerity, nor the depth of his feelings. They were everything she had hoped for when she wondered if he knew he could lose her forever.

She stumbled up the steps into the keep and found herself at Muireall's door before she realized where she was going.

Muireall stood as she stormed in. "Ella?"

Somehow, along the way, she found her voice. "Is Euan here?"

"Nay, he went to the training ground to watch the lads."

"I dinna ken what to do. Yet I do. Calum has my heart, and I have naught to give to any other man." She stopped talking, breath sawing from her lungs, in and out.

Muireall took her arm and led her to a seat by the hearth.

"What happened, Ella? Ye are upset."

"Calum. Calum happened. He gave me everything I wanted from him. His words, ach, the things he said. I'll never forget them. Calum has my heart, nay other."

"And what did ye say to him in return?"

A knot formed in her throat that she couldn't swallow. She tried to clear it, shaking her head as she did so, not certain how she could still breathe around it. But she did. She simply couldn't speak.

Muireall crossed her arms, frowning. "Ye ran, did ye? And ye came here?"

She nodded, unable to do more.

"Ye say Calum has yer heart. Lass, it does ye nay good to tell me. Ye must find yer voice and tell him. Go to him. If ye want yer happiness and the life ye both want together to happen, ye canna stay here. I want ye both to be happy. And seeing ye happy together is the best thing I could hope for."

Tears flooded Ella's eyes. She bit back a sob behind her fist and nodded. She had to leave before she embarrassed herself any further. She stood, nodding and managed to whisper, "Thank ye," before she fled from her friend's concerned gaze. Where was Calum? Surely not still in the walled garden. Where would he go after she ran from him. He must think she'd refused him. She would find him. And she would make things right between them. He'd done his part. Now it was her turn.

CALUM HAD WATCHED Ella run from him in disbelief. He followed her for a few steps, but then stopped. Chasing her, stopping her when she so clearly wanted to get away from him would do no good. His belly roiled and he feared he'd lose his last meal on a nearby rose bush, but he swallowed and fought the urge down.

He'd thought his world ended when he woke up blind and lived through weeks more in darkness. He'd had no idea the depth of devastation he had yet to feel. How could she repay the hurt he'd done to her so shockingly? So viciously. And so finally. His words meant nothing to her. His apology, his love, his offer of marriage were worthless. Surely now she would accept any betrothal offer Iain offered, and leave Brodie as quickly as could be arranged.

His feet seemed mired in mud. He couldn't take the next step. He stood, staring at a pink rose, the shade of Ella's lips, so perfect in form and color that it brought tears to his eyes. Perfect and beautiful, like Ella. And like her, laced with thorns that stripped the skin from his body, the flesh from his heart. He reached out and grabbed the stem, snapping it, and then crushed the rose in his other hand. When he let the petals fall, he was surprised to see bloody streaks in his palm and bits of thorns embedded at the top of each. He hadn't felt a thing except the frozen void in his chest where his heart used to be.

He clenched the hand into a fist, ignoring the sting and forced himself to move. One foot in front of the other, one after another, until he reached the garden gate. He stopped there and slammed his hand into the solid oaken door, wanting the pain to mask the shuddering sensation around the frigid hole in his chest.

He should have gone after her. He should have done many things. But the one thing he should not have done was take out his fury and fear of his injuries on Ella. He'd destroyed any hope of ever having her love. Of a life with her. He pounded the gate again and again until his knuckles bled as freely as the thorn punctures in his palm. Seeing that much blood stopped him. He was a fool. He'd been about to ruin his hand and risk the one future left to him as a Brodie warrior and scout. Yet, without Ella, was any of it worth anything?

Disgusted with himself, he made his way to the herbal to get the healer to clean up the mess he'd made. Ella wouldn't be there. As upset as she'd been, she'd go to her chamber or to Muireall's. If only Mhairi could also heal broken hearts. He knew of two who could use her help.

Ella intercepted him before he reached the keep's door. "Calum! I found ye. God's bones, what happened to yer hand? Ye are bleeding."

He fought back the answer he'd been tempted to give: "Ye did." She happened to his hand. But that wasn't true. He had done this. He lost control. "'Tis naught," he bit out. "What do ye need now?" He couldn't help the bitterness of his tone. What was she doing here?

She drew back from it, but after a moment, straightened and a determined light glowed in her eyes.

"Ye, Calum. I need ye. I'm sorry I ran. I...yer words meant so much to me, I couldna breathe, couldna think. I could only feel. Too much. I...I feared my heart would burst and I didna want to die in front of ye." She pressed her hands to her chest and shook her head as she ran out of words. "That sounds foolish now, I ken it."

"So ye are saying I hurt ye again?"

"Nay, Calum. Ye misunderstand me. My heart was so full, I didna ken what to do with all the wonderful feelings. Yer words gave me...everything I ever hoped to hear from ye. Everything I hoped we could be again. And more. I shouldna have run as I did."

Hope was a cruel thing. It bloomed in Calum's chest like the rose he'd just destroyed. The perfect, beautiful rose. Thorns and all, like Ella, perfect and flawed, and the one woman in the world he loved. Her eyes shone with emotion. Her hands reached for him, but she clenched them and held fast before touching him. He wanted her touch. He wanted to touch her. More than anything, he wanted her in his arms. But could he trust what he was feeling, much less what she professed to be feeling? They'd been at cross-purposes before. Did they truly understand each other now? He hoped so. More than he'd ever hoped for anything else. Only one thing she could say would convince him the hope blossoming in his chest wouldn't destroy him.

"If Iain gave ye the chance, would ye accept another betrothal offer?"

Her eyes filled as she gazed up at him. "From ye, aye. Only ye. Ye have my heart, Calum. There will be nay other for me." She reached out again and this time, she laid her hand over the frozen spot in his chest. Magically, it warmed and eased, and he felt his heart beating again within it. "If I understood ye, I have yers." With her other hand, she pressed her own chest. "We are joined in some way. Meant to be together."

"So ye will marry me?"

"I will. Freely and happily, I will marry ye. And we will make a good life together."

EPILOGUE

"Euan is so grateful ye postponed yer wedding until he was able to stand with Calum as his best man," Muireall told Ella a week later.

"It wasna a difficult decision. He's Calum's best friend, as ye are mine. We needed both of ye with us as we take this step."

"Still, ye didna have to do it, and I'm grateful for Euan's sake. Ye are good friends to both of us."

"And havena ye been the same to Calum and me?"

Muireall laughed at that. "Aye, ye have a point. Ach, ye are such a bonnie bride. I canna wait for Calum to see ye."

Ella smoothed her simple blue dress, the Munro plaid she'd brought from home pinned at her right shoulder. It hung along her torso front and back. After the priest blessed their union, Calum would drape the Brodie tartan over her left shoulder and across her heart. Muireall would tie it at her waist on the other side, celebrating her new ties to Brodie and to him, but leaving the Munro plaid in place under it to acknowledge the clan she came from.

Friends from Rose and other nearby clans were here to show their support. No one from Ross had been invited, though. Ella appreciated the thought behind that.

Someone knocked on the chamber door. Muireall went to answer it while Ella turned her back. If it was Calum, he should not see her before she reached the kirk. After a low murmur of conversation, Muireall closed the door.

"'Twas Kenneth," she said as Ella turned to face her. "They're ready for us at the kirk. Are ye ready?"

Ella smiled, anticipation lifting her spirits, making her more excited than she'd felt in months, save perhaps, for the day Calum finally gave her his heart and asked for her hand. "I am. I canna wait to become Calum's wife."

Muireall opened the door and gestured Ella through it. "'Twillna be long now."

The walk down the steps to the great hall, then outside and around the keep's towers through the bailey to the clan's wee kirk seemed to take forever. Ella took deep breaths, trying to slow her heart's frantic beating, and to notice everything around her. The blue of the sky, the tang of salt in the breeze from the Moray Firth. She recalled all the things Calum had noted as she'd walked with him in the bailey the first day he'd been allowed outside while his eyes were still covered. That day seemed eons ago. They'd been through so much. And now, it was all about to come together into the life and the family she'd dreamed of. That they'd both longed for, even when they couldn't admit it to themselves, much less to each other.

Finally the kirk came into view, a crowd gathered before it made up of friends and family. And on the steps, Father Innis, Calum and Euan. Annie and Cat, Iain and Georgie stood watching her and Muireall approach from just below the steps.

Both men had smiles of anticipation on their faces, Calum's brighter and broader than she'd ever seen him wear. She had no doubt the smile she gave him was just as bright, just as happy, and just as eager for their marriage to take place. Even Muireall's brother grinned at her, excitement lighting his eyes.

She mounted the steps and Calum held out his hand, reaching for her. Everything around her disappeared save for him, eager to touch her, to wed her.

"Ye are the bonniest bride in all of Scotland," he told her, pulling her up beside him and bending to kiss her hand. "I'm a lucky man."

Euan's chuckle broke the bubble that seemed to surround her and Calum. "I'm glad ye finally saw what was right in front of yer eyes, Calum."

Ella groaned, unsure how Calum would react to that unsubtle reminder of his injury, but he chuckled, so she laughed, too.

"It took me too long," Calum said, his expression turning serious as he regarded her, "and nearly cost me everything. But Ella, I must ask ye again if ye are certain ye want a man like me when ye could have yer pick of any man in Brodie? Or anywhere else, for that matter. Iain was right about that. We will only do this if it is what ye truly want."

"I want ye, Calum, to be my husband for the rest of my life. For all of our lives." Her thoughts tumbled for a moment to the marriage she had escaped. Calum was not the same as Thomas Ross. She did not want to inject the Ross name into this moment. "The past doesna matter. The future does. Ye are everything to me."

"And ye are everything to me. Despite how that realization scared me and made me do foolish things, I finally learned that I am more afraid of living without ye."

"Dinna fash, love. Ye willna. My life starts now, with the man I see before me, and the future ye show me."

"Then let us begin," Calum said and turned with her to face the priest.

She didn't hear most of what Father Innis said. She replied, making her vows only with Calum's help, his hand holding hers giving it a little squeeze when it was time for her to speak. Finally, the priest declared them man and wife. After Calum draped the Brodie tartan over her left shoulder and across her heart, he took her in his arms and kissed her in front of all their well-wishers. Once the cheering died down, they entered the kirk for the wedding blessing before returning to the great hall for the celebration Iain and Annie arranged for them.

The clan's laird and lady offered their congratulations first. "We're so happy for ye both," Annie said.

Calum met Iain's gaze. "Were ye really expecting a betrothal offer for Ella to arrive soon?"

Iain smiled. "I lied."

Before this day, Calum might have taken offense.

Another lie. And not a small one, like the many he'd observed when he discovered everyone but him knew about the Janet ruse. Iain risked much. Ella might have taken him at his word and asked for a match away from Brodie. Calum might have done something rash. Right now, he couldn't think what, except that surely Euan would have been involved and there would have been trouble for all of them. But now, healed and blissfully married, he found he could say, "I am very glad ye did," and mean every word of it.

Annie grabbed him and kissed his cheek. "Ye were stubborn, Calum, but worth the trouble. Still, Ella has her work cut out for her, living with ye."

"And I'll enjoy every moment of it," Ella said, having overheard Annie's last comment after being distracted by Muireall and Euan joining them. "What are we talking about?"

"Unless I miss my guess," Euan said, "yer stubborn husband. If we all hadna taken him in hand, I dinna ken if we'd be here right now."

"Nay, Euan," Muireall interrupted, poking him in the ribs with her elbow. "We canna take credit for this. Calum and Ella both made this decision. The right one. Though we werena certain they ever would."

Several hours later, the food, drink, dancing and excitement took their toll. Ella was ready to leave the party.

Calum took her hand and stood. "'Tis time for us to go to our chamber, my wife."

"Gladly, my husband," she told him with a smile and

rose to her feet beside him. "I'm ready for ye to make me yer wife in all ways."

"Ye will tell me if ye are at all uncomfortable, aye? I dinna wish—"

"All will be well, husband. I trust ye to care for me."

"And I love ye beyond reason, Ella. We will see many happy years together, starting tonight. I promise ye that and more."

"Yer love is all I need, husband, for me to have everything I have longed for. With ye."

"Damn it, I dinna need the healer!" Euan's voice echoed down the hallway from the great hall a fortnight after the wedding.

Ella, recently accepted and confirmed as the healer's apprentice, glanced at Mhairi and shrugged. "Nay doubt he was on the practice field again. Muireall will no' be pleased."

The healer nodded as Calum pushed Euan ahead of him into the herbal. "Sit yerself down, lad," she directed with a stern look as she noted the blood on Euan's sleeve. "What happened?"

"He willna listen," Calum said before Euan could defend himself.

"Doing too much again, aye? Ella, see to him."

Surprise lifted Euan's brow.

"I'm the apprentice," Ella told him. "With full authority to bind yer arm to yer side if ye dinna stop yer foolishness."

She pulled the blood-soaked sleeve away from his skin as Calum stepped forward to untie his leine and shove the neck wide enough to expose the cut Euan had spent weeks healing. Blood welled from a new cut just below it. "Ach, Euan, this isna the same wound."

"Nay, 'tis another, damn it. One of the lads got a wee bit carried away with being given his first real blade."

"'Twasna Georgie, was it?"

Calum shook his head. "Nay, an older lad did this." He frowned at Euan. "I told ye they were no' ready for those blades," he said.

Euan simply growled in response.

Ella bit back a laugh as she cleaned the wound and inspected it. "Despite the blood, 'tis no' too deep. It will heal well—if ye let it."

Calum, at her back, snorted. "I guess that means I'm in charge of training the lads again."

"Ye are the apprentice arms master," Euan reminded him. "So next time, ye will be the one sitting here…ach!" He gave Ella a pained stare, brow wrinkled over slitted eyes. "While yer wife tortures ye. I'll look forward to seeing that."

"*Wheesht!*" Ella demanded. "I'm no' torturing ye. I'm making sure this wound doesna fester."

"Dinna complain," the healer interjected, "or I'll make sure yer wife kens how ye've been greetin'. Annie's wean makes less noise than ye."

"Greetin'!" Euan barked out his objection to being characterized as crying like a baby.

Calum roared with laughter.

"Ye and Calum are cut from the same cloth," Ella told both men. "Stubborn, and poor patients. Mayhap I should rethink being the healer's apprentice."

The healer, on the other side of the chamber, cleared her throat. "Or mayhap nay."

"It seems we both have our path decided for us," Calum told her and leaned in to kiss her cheek.

"Aye, well, ye are still a Brodie scout, yer greatest wish. What do I get to do to make up for dealing with cantankerous patients like this one?" She asked and tilted her head at Euan. Her hands were busy binding his arm.

"Ye, lass, were my greatest wish. But as to the other, let me think…helping to decorate the hall for the midwinter solstice feast?"

Ella snorted, her gaze firmly fixed on what she was doing to Euan's wound. "Good try. What about the rest of the year?"

"Being wife and lover to me, ye bonnie lass," Calum told her, kissing her cheek once again. "That should be enough to make any lass ecstatically happy."

Euan coughed so hard, Ella was afraid for him. Then he broke into a grin.

"Like to live dangerously, do ye, Calum?"

Ella elbowed her husband away when he leaned toward her again. "Go on with ye. Euan doesna need ye to supervise. Nor do I." Then she turned fully to him and kissed him. "I'll see ye in our chamber later, husband. Be more careful than yer friend, here, so I dinna have to tend to ye in this one."

Calum grinned. "Aye, and I will look forward to it. Being tended to in our chamber, that is. No' this one."

THE HEARTH FIRE in their chamber burned down to embers by the time Calum tucked Ella against his side. She breathed softly and evenly, already drifting into slumber, warm and safe and sated. He took a breath, still awed by the love they now shared. Getting past his stubbornness and both their reluctance to trust the person they loved had been a hard-fought battle. For him, at least. He'd learned his pride was a dangerous thing, keeping him from the happiness he needed and she deserved. She'd stood by him after his injury, stubborn enough in her own way to need to be part of his healing, and knowing better than he that he needed her there. As herself and as Janet, the side of her not afraid to be stern with him, or to stand up to him. To do what his sweet Ella, at that time, could not do herself.

"I love ye, lass," he murmured into her hair. "Both of ye. Both sides of ye saved me."

"Both...what are ye babbling about, love?" She roused and rose up on her elbow to look at him with eyes full of slumber and a face so lovely it hurt to look upon her. Yet her visage was not as lovely as her heart. Her spirit.

"Ye, as ye, and as Janet. Ye saved more than my sight, ye ken. Ye saved my life. And, perhaps, my soul. I was broken, and ye wouldna let me remain that way. I owe ye everything, my wife. Both of ye."

"Janet wasna real, husband."

"Aye, she was." He took her hand and ran his thumb from wrist to fingertips and back again. "She was the part of ye that ye couldna show to anyone but me, because I needed her the most. She sacrificed her beautiful hands to convince me she was someone I could trust. She didna let me wallow in myself. I love my sweet Ella, but I also love my stern, determined Janet. They're both ye, love. And they're both safe with me. I never want ye to harm yerself again for me."

She tightened her fingers over his thumb. "My hands healed, Calum. They're fine now."

He lifted hers to his lips and dropped a kiss on her delicate wrist. "Aye, they are."

"And if ye need her again, will ye welcome Janet's return?"

"Dinna ye mean *when* I need her again? Surely I will."

"Verra well, when…"

"I've learned my lesson, love. I may no' welcome the need for her, but I will welcome her."

"Then that is enough. For both of us. And perhaps there are more sides to me that ye have yet to experience?"

"Aye? Such as?"

She brushed her fingers gently across his upper chest, then lower. "I have learned much from ye, husband."

His belly tightened with anticipation.

"But there is still more to learn. To experience. To love about ye."

"'Tis glad I am that ye think so," he managed to mumble,

deep in his chest, as her hand drifted to his belly. "What else would ye like to learn?"

"All there is to ken, love, about loving ye. Pleasing ye."

"Nay more than I wish to learn all there is to ken about pleasing ye, Ella. 'Tis my greatest wish at the moment." He sucked in a breath as her hand slipped lower. "And forever."

She gave him a saucy smile, full of both sweet Ella and determined Janet. "Then let us begin."

Highland Talents Heritage

Highland Prodigy

Highland Memories

Highland Reckoning

Highland Dreamer

Highland Echo

His Highland Heart

His Highland Rose

His Highland Heart

His Highland Love

His Highland Bride

Laird of Lies

Laird of Sighs

Her Highland Deception

His Highland Heart Boxed Set

Highland Talents

Heart of Stone

Highland Healer

The Healer's Gift

When Highland Lightning Strikes

Highland Seer

Highland Troth

Lost Love

Waiting for the Laird

Waiting for a Forever Love

Other Novels

Highland Seasons

Highland Beginnings

ABOUT THE AUTHOR

Willa Blair is an award-winning Amazon and Barnes and Noble #1 bestselling author of Scottish historical, light paranormal, and contemporary romance filled with men in kilts, psi talents, and plenty of spice. Her books have won numerous accolades, including the Marlene, Merritt, National Readers' Choice Award Finalist, Booksellers' Best Award Finalist, National Excellence of Romance Fiction Awards Finalist, National Excellence in Story Telling Award Finalist, Romance Through the Ages Contest Finalist, Reader's Crown finalist, InD'Tale Magazine's RONE Award Honorable Mention, and NightOwl Reviews Top Picks. She loves reading and writing novels set in the past, present, and future, as well as scouting new settings for books. She has visited six continents and can get by in several languages. She thinks being an author is the best job she's ever had.

Willa loves hearing from readers!
Contact her:
www.willablair.com
authorwillablair@gmail.com

Sign up for my Newsletter
Find links to the rest of my books

OLIVERHEBERBOOKS

A small press bound by the belief that every voice matters.

Sign up for our newsletter to learn about new releases and more.
https://oliver-heberbooks.com/subscribe/

Follow us on social media:

facebook.com/oliverheberbooks
instagram.com/oliverheberbooks
amazon.com/oliverheberbooks
youtube.com/@OliverHeberBooksPublisher